T0132467

Cosmic Kitty

A Mindful, Metaphysical Journey

Shan Gill

BALBOA.
PRESS

A DIVISION OF HAY HOUSE

Balboa Press books may be ordered through booksellers or by contacting:

Balboa Press
A Division of Hay House
1663 Liberty Drive
Bloomington, IN 47403
www.balboapress.com
1 (877) 407-4847

Because of the dynamic nature of the Internet, any web addresses or
links contained in this book may have changed since publication and
may no longer be valid. The views expressed in this work are solely those
of the author and do not necessarily reflect the views of the publisher,
and the publisher hereby disclaims any responsibility for them.

The author of this book does not dispense medical advice or prescribe the use
of any technique as a form of treatment for physical, emotional, or medical
problems without the advice of a physician, either directly or indirectly. The
intent of the author is only to offer information of a general nature to help
you in your quest for emotional and spiritual well-being. In the event you use
any of the information in this book for yourself, which is your constitutional
right, the author and the publisher assume no responsibility for your actions.

Print information available on the last page.

ISBN: 978-1-5043-6914-5 (sc)
ISBN: 978-1-5043-6916-9 (hc)
ISBN: 978-1-5043-6915-2 (e)

Library of Congress Control Number: 2016918409

Balboa Press rev. date: 01/25/2017

CONTENTS

DEDICATION

This book is dedicated to James and Adair, my nephew and niece, ages 5 and 3, at the time of this writing. My hope for them, and all children, is that they will remain open to the knowledge they bring with them into this world. May they continue to see and speak with the angels, fairies, loved ones, and other beings of light here to support us throughout our lives; may they continue to have a direct connection with their Guides and never be shut down by adults who can no longer see or feel the magic; may this and all generations of children remind and teach we adults what it means to truly have faith and trust in God, the Universe, or whomever guides us.

This book is also dedicated to those children and adults who are still open and honest in recognizing that we only see and feel a small portion of what's around us; unless we listen and pay attention. What are your Guides and Angels telling you? Listen closely... You may just find a path to a whole new world...

Chapter 1

WELCOME TO JOY-VILLE

I t was a gray, overcast morning in Joy-Ville, and no one could figure out why. The Sun was hiding behind heavy, dark clouds, a very unusual place for him. Normally he would come out first thing every morning to start the new day. The residents of Joy-Ville were curious about his absence, but they were not concerned. You see, worry does not exist in Joy-Ville, not really. Certainly, if someone went missing or something happened that required action, the neighbors would jump in to help and figure out what could be done. But concern about the future was not a big priority for the town and hadn't been for hundreds and hundreds of years.

Centuries ago, the residents of Joy-Ville made a decision. They decided to change the way they lived. They wanted a place of peace and harmony, as they were very tired of the anger, fear, and violence around them. They even re-named their town to call it "Joy-Ville", to remind them each day of what they intended to create together.

And because of these intentions and actions, Joy-Ville became a beautiful place. It was filled with green rolling hills, flowers, and trees everywhere, and vibrant colors, almost like cartoons in their clarity and brilliance. The vibration was high and the air clean and nourishing. A good day in Joy-Ville just made you feel, well, *joyful* and also content; you couldn't help it. The energy was very positive, and things were calm. Life was good. The beings who lived in Joy-Ville did not worry; they did what they loved and followed their life purpose. They worked in jobs that provided great satisfaction and generally had an easy and fulfilling way of life. Joy-Ville residents lived a long time with few illnesses and spent a lot of time in meditation. They learned from each other and especially from those who were much older and wiser. The residents in this land lived in harmony with nature. In fact, they even worked to communicate with the animals, flowers, and trees as part of their daily life. It was a wonderful way to live.

Even with all this happiness, the people of Joy-Ville liked routine and knowing what would happen next. They enjoyed going about their long, easy, peaceful lives with no surprises and few changes. So a gray, overcast morning where the Sun did not come out and say "hello" felt a little awkward for most of the residents, because it changed up their day. Except one. She didn't mind change one bit. She craved adventure, so a different start to the day was refreshing. Her name was Cosmic Kitty.

Cosmic Kitty (CK to her friends) was a very special being, with more curiosity than most of her friends and neighbors. This lovely girl had sparkling green eyes, mops of curly bright red hair and pink freckles on her pale face. She was like any other young girl, playful and full of life. However, she had a few unusual characteristics as well. For example, her head was shaped like a heart (to match her inner spirit) and she also had short black whiskers that protruded out from her round black button nose. Cosmic Kitty stood on two legs, as a typical person does. She had two arms, two hands, a torso, a neck and all the normal parts that come with walking upright and talking and living in a "human" world. Except for her heart-shaped head and whiskers, she would look pretty normal - in a typical "humanoid" way. What was different about Cosmic Kitty was her energy. You could see it. Her blue and green and gold aura surrounded her. You could literally see the parts of her that were more than her physical body.

For those not familiar with the term, the aura is the shell of energy that surrounds all beings. It is the energy we create and send out to others. It is part of the natural essence of who we are. The color of something or someone's aura can tell you how they feel, their purpose in life, what kind of spirit or being they are and many other things.

Most of us don't see this aura. But Cosmic Kitty's aura was shiny and bright for all to see! This was normal in Joy-Ville, as everything had an energy field that could be seen by others. Her family, her friends, the trees, mountains, animals – everything. The color and quality of the aura were just part of what everyone saw on each other. It was just as normal as looking at someone's teeth or noticing the color of their eyes. When someone described another in her world, it usually included a description of the energy color that surrounded them. So Cosmic Kitty would be described as the girl with red hair, green eyes, a heart-shaped head, whiskers and a blue and green aura. It was just the usual thing to do.

Cosmic Kitty loved living in Joy-Ville. She and her friends would play games, meditate and study. They would gather together with Mr. Tortoise, one of the oldest and wisest of beings, and they would be amazed and awestruck as he spoke of far-off places and tales of times very long ago when their ancestors walked the land. The young pupils would listen intently, absorbed in every word, as Mr. Tortoise spoke of times when the energy in their land was not so positive, people did not always get along, and they actually had something called "violence"! Cosmic Kitty and her friends had a hard time imagining people arguing, much less hurting each other! They didn't understand where that kind of behavior might come from and why it seemed necessary. They also heard stories of how other lands are out beyond their world, and how time does not really exist. The students did not always believe every story Mr. Tortoise told, but it often made for a fun afternoon and lively discussion of learning.

When not studying, playing with her friends, meditating or doing other activities, Cosmic Kitty would often walk through the hills near her home and talk to the flowers, birds and other animals who lived around her. And they would usually speak back, in whatever way they could. She was also friends with the sun and moon, naming them "Sunny" and "Moon Man".

Cosmic Kitty had a very special gift of communicating with nature. She was able to understand, feel and hear other beings more so than other residents of Joy-Ville. So when she was out walking, it was not unusual to see her in deep conversation with a small animal, a tree or even looking up at the sky speaking to the sun. She had a very special talent that she practiced every day. And today was no exception. She decided to go for a walk, even though her friend Sunny had not yet come out.

As morning turned into lunchtime, Sunny finally decided to emerge.

"Good afternoon, Sunny!" said CK, as her friend began to shine from around some nearby clouds.

In a deep, caring voice that only CK could hear and understand, Sunny replied, "CK, how are you? Lovely to see you today!"

"We missed you this morning, my friend," CK said.

"I know," Sunny replied, "I was sleepy and decided to rest."

"All good," replied CK, "we love to see you, but it's fun to have a little change as well. Glad you got some rest!" CK exclaimed.

Sunny winked at her as she walked past, showing that he knew she was off for a good walk and perhaps an adventure, as she had a habit of doing.

As CK strolled along the path, she came upon a large pond. She could see Sunny's reflection on the pond as she walked by, rays of yellow and gold light shining across the water. She could see the fish and young turtles swimming together through the clear surface, playing games of tag under the shimmer of Sunny's bright rays. The fish came in several different colors, mainly because of their different auras and energy. But most were large orange goldfish, with big eyes. A few were black and green in color, with a school of silvery white ones as well. The young turtles would come up behind the fish, very slowly and quietly, and reaching out ever so gently with their mouths, they would lightly nip the tail of an unsuspecting fish, indicating "Tag! You're It!" The fish, often caught by surprise, would turn around quickly. Some would scowl at the young turtles with disapproving eyes, but most would engage in play, tagging other turtles or other fish into the game. Most were happy to join in. Only a few older fish did not want to play but were tolerant of the younger ones who had been energized by the Sun's rays.

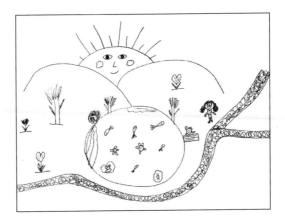

As CK rounded the edge of the pond, her friends the frogs sat at the water's edge, singing their songs of "croak" to each other. The different tones made by the frogs worked in harmony for a joyous song. A few of the frogs continued to do the backstroke, swimming across the pond, going from lily pad to lily pad. Some of the turtles had pulled themselves up out of the water, lying on top of logs, warming their shells in the newly emerging rays. It was a good day – full of joy and warmth, much like many other days in Joy-Ville.

Cosmic Kitty spoke to the frogs as she passed. "Beautiful voices," she complimented, "thanks for the great tune!"

One of the frogs blushed, in a way that only frogs can. He smiled under his froggy cheeks, turning to jump into the water with his buddies. CK wondered if any of them needed to be kissed. She had read many stories about how kissing a frog might turn him into a handsome prince and release him from whatever spell he might be under. She laughed at the idea, as she continued to round the corner of the pond's edge.

As she emerged on the backside of the pond, one of her favorite Frog friends, Timrek, was sitting on a log.

"Ah, Timrek," Cosmic Kitty greeted him. "How are you?"

"Any better and I couldn't stand it," replied the green frog. CK could tell he was deep in thought. A dreamy look covered his eyes as he looked towards the sky. Timrek had his favorite banjo sitting on his lap, ready to play whenever inspiration might strike. But for now, he was content to watch the clouds roll by and wonder what they might be covering up.

As CK slowly walked past him, her mind began to wander as well. She began to think about typical things that girls think about. She wondered what her friends were doing. She was curious about Sunny and Moon Man, of course. But mostly she daydreamed about her friend in the sky, Starlight, and what was happening past the dark boundaries of space.

CK had heard that perhaps her world was not the only one. Kind voices in her head, and a feeling in her heart made her believe that perhaps other worlds existed that she could not see or touch, but they were there. Many of these worlds were on other planets in her Universe, and some were even further out. Mr. Tortoise had said that some of these worlds even lived in different dimensions! He had tried to explain to Cosmic Kitty how all matter is just energy and that the frequency or vibration of that energy determines what it turns into and how it feels. He told CK that the higher the dimension, the higher the vibration of the place the beings in that dimension lived! It was an interesting concept for CK, even though she did not fully grasp all the mechanics behind it. But as she daydreamed about what might live past her friend Starlight, she wondered about those beings on the other planets and what they might be up to right now.

Walking along with her head in the clouds, CK could hear Timrek begin to sing a familiar and favorite song that was passed down from generations of frogs over many centuries. The song was called "Rainbow Connection."*

CK loved this song so much she had even made up her own words to go with it and she quietly began to sing her own version while listening to Timrek sing in the distance...

"How are there so many cosmic connections,
and where do the moonbeams go?

How do we understand what is inside us,
and all of the ways we grow?

Some say we should be alone on this planet;
That's just not true for today.

Someday they'll find us, our cosmic connections,
and Angels will show us the way.

Starlight and moonbeams, they live all around us
and show us the way to go home.

During our dream time, they bring in the Cosmos
and from this sweet dreamland we roam.

How is our real life so deep and fulfilling
and yet we still question the gray?

Someday they'll find us, our cosmic connections,
and Angels will show us the way.

---

* "Rainbow Connection" was first performed in The Muppet Movie by Jim Henson and Kermit the Frog in 1979

All of us full of its love,
We know we are filled with its magic….

Calling to each of us, hearing the heartbeat,
I know they live so close by,
Wanting to reach for us, share in this lifetime,
but we aren't so sure we know why.

The voice in my heart is too clear to ignore it;
It says they want to come play.

Someday they'll find us, our cosmic connections,
and Angels will show us the way.

La, la la, La, la la la, La Laa, la la, La, La la laaaaaaa…"

As she sang, Cosmic Kitty continued to meander along the path, and in daydreaming of far-off places and distant lands, she was not watching her direction. She had learned to "be present" long ago and pay attention to where she was going and the energy around it, but today she was not. She veered off the path and into an area close to where the large mountains live. When she finally stopped daydreaming about Cosmic Connections and Starlight, she realized she had walked all the way to Whale Mountain!

Whale Mountain was called that because the rock had formed into the shape of a whale. One side went straight up from the ground, forming the whale's huge head, and then it began to slope back along one edge like the top and body of a long whale. A crack in the rock towards the base gave the rock a slight smile like it knew a secret that no one else knew. Whale Mountain always held an interesting feeling around it – open, yet secretive. No one knew how long the mountain had been there, just that it had always looked like a whale and provided shelter for animals at different times of the year.

As CK slowly woke up from her daydream, she noticed something unusual. For the first time ever, just above the crack that looked like a smile, CK saw a small swirling area. It almost looked like the eye of the whale. It seemed to be going around in a circle, and the effect made the side of the mountain seem to come alive visibly. The swirl became transparent, and looking straight into the mountain, CK could see something on the other side.

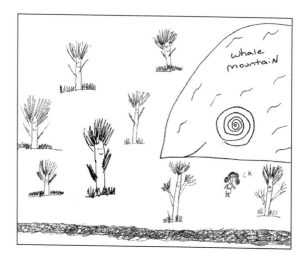

At first, she was perplexed, and CK asked herself, "Why can I see through the mountain? That's odd. And why is it blurry? Like it's vibrating?"

Though this seemed strange and unusual, CK was not afraid. In her world, there was little to be afraid of. She was always protected and taken care of. The other beings with whom she shared Joy-Ville were respectful and peaceful. Even when an accident did occur, and someone was hurt, most of the beings in Joy-Ville knew how to call upon healing energy called Reiki to instantly heal whatever the body had experienced. So she had no reason to be concerned.

CK decided to get a closer look and check it out. As she walked up toward the swirling portal, it was obvious this was not a typical little whirlwind like one might see in the desert areas. The side of the mountain was actually spinning in a spiral formation! She remembered something Mr. Tortoise had told her long ago. He said their world had several portals that would link them to other worlds and other dimensions.

"We don't know exactly where they are located or where they go, but these portals were used in ancient times to travel. However, our ancestors stopped using them, though we were never sure why. And eventually everyone forgot about them," Mr. Tortoise had told her.

CK looked into the swirling portal on the side of the mountain, and she began to dream that perhaps this was her way to visit her friend Starlight directly! Maybe she could meet some new friends and find out who lived on those planets she knew were out there! Maybe she could see some other places too!?

While she loved her home and all of her friends, Cosmic Kitty craved adventure. She wanted to see new places and new experiences outside of her small home. She wanted to try new things and meet new people. With a deep breath and great determination, she bravely stepped forward into the spinning portal.

Chapter 2

THE THIRD DIMENSION

Cosmic Kitty walked a few steps and then found herself coming out the other side of the mountain. As she looked around, the scenery had changed quite a bit. Although it was still the same mountain on the other side, the colors were not as bright as the green grass and clean air in her world. It was a bit more "hazy" in color, a bit duller. The trees were not as green, and they did not speak to her.

Cosmic Kitty said out loud, "How odd! Why are the trees not saying 'hello'?"

A familiar voice came to CK's ears, a voice of wisdom and comfort. "Because my dear, these are not your trees. In this world, the trees don't talk."

Cosmic Kitty looked up and was startled to see that, for the first time, there was a body that went with this voice she had heard since she was a baby. Hanging slightly above her, there floated a glowing being. She had a heart-shaped head, just like Cosmic Kitty, but she had gray hair and large, gentle brown eyes. She hovered a few feet above the ground, dressed in a white robe with a cute belt and pearl earrings. It was CK's grandmother – Nana Whiskers!

CK could not believe it! She had never actually met her grandmother, but she saw pictures of her when she was young. CK was astonished that this was the voice she had heard for years! She just assumed it was her "inner dialogue" and one part of her personality was always giving her good ideas and wisdom beyond her age. Of course, as Mr. Tortoise had always said, even our guardian angels and departed loved ones are all part of the cosmic divine universe – we are all linked together through God. So in a way, it WAS part of her inner voice. However, at this moment, Cosmic Kitty was not thinking about divine connections between souls or even how God and the Universe work. At this moment she was both surprised and relieved to see Nana Whiskers floating beside her.

Even though she had never actually met her grandmother, everything in her heart told her this being was her spirit. Mr. Tortoise would say this was "claircognizance" - a very big word that means a "sense of knowing." But right now CK didn't need a sense of knowing. She could see and hear her grandmother directly in front of her. And once she got over the shock, she was very excited!

"What are you doing here?!?" Cosmic Kitty almost screamed.

"I am often here, dear one, looking out for you, providing guidance, taking walks with you. I am always around," said Nana Whiskers calmly.

"But why can I see you now?" asked CK.

"Because we are in another dimension of your life. The vibration is lower in this dimension, but since your vibration is higher than the environment in this dimension, you can see me here," said Nana Whiskers.

Cosmic Kitty got a confused look on her face, squinting her eyes and nose at her grandmother. With great patience, CK's grandmother continued to explain.

"You see, all of us have many different lives going on at the same time. They are happening in parallel universes. We are all made up of energy, and parts of our energy can be in different places at the same time. Some of our energy acts as our soul, combined with a body and mind and personality to create us in this world so that we can experience life. But when that happens, we can have multiple versions of the same body, mind, and soul living on different planes."

CK continued to look confused, raising an eyebrow at her grandmother.

"Think of it this way. Picture blocks stacked and each level is a dimension or individual world.* The higher blocks resemble upper

---

* Dimension blocks analogy inspired by Larry Flaxman, "The Grid" and his analogy of dimensions being floors in a building.

dimensions, and the bottom blocks are the lower dimensions. The life you know today is actually in what's called the fifth dimension. The vibration and energy are quite high. There is a great deal of love in the air, and we understand and respect each other and live in harmony with our world. We are considered to be living on one of the blocks closer to the Heavens, closer to the Angels and closer to the spirit realm. That is one of the reasons you can hear your other guardians and me so clearly when you are at home. That is also why you can speak with the other parts of nature, and they can hear you as well," explained Nana Whiskers.

"The world you have just entered through that portal is another version of your life. It is the same lifetime, but this world is actually on a lower level of the blocks. It is a lower dimension. The energy and vibrations are not as positive and strong as the world you come from. This version of your world is sitting in the third dimension."

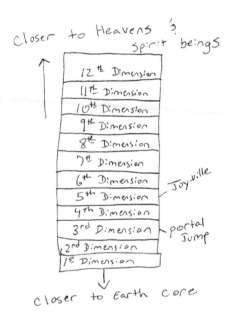

CK's head reeled with all of this information – it was a lot to absorb! Not only were there other worlds and planets as she had hoped; there were also different versions of her own lifetime as well. WOW! This revelation was huge! She wondered if Mr. Tortoise knew about that part. She would have to tell him when she got back.

Nana Whiskers continued to explain. "The reason the color looks more hazy here and the trees do not talk to you is that even though this world is similar to your world in appearance, it is also very different regarding how everyone grew up, their beliefs, the environment, etc... Your friends may be here, but they were born and grew up in a very different energy and vibration, as did the *You* who lives in this dimension as well."

"I know that is a lot to understand, but that is why you can see me now. I can exist in all of the dimensions, both your fifth dimension and this third dimension version of our world. Since you come from a world where higher vibration is normal, you can see me and others who exist on that higher vibration plane when you are in this world. So essentially, I am at a vibration where you can actually see me because YOU are also living at a higher vibration than this world. Does that make sense?" asked Nana Whiskers.

"Sort of," said CK, who by this time had taken a seat on a nearby rock to keep from passing out with information overload. It was overwhelming. "So are you saying that the reason I can see you here and not in my world is that in my world your vibration is higher than the fifth dimension and so you are harder for me to see there? But in this world, your vibration is lower than when you are in Joy-Ville. Therefore, since my vibration is high from living in Joy-Ville (which is in the fifth dimension), I can see you because you had to lower your vibration here in the third dimension?"

"Precisely!" clapped Nana Whiskers, bringing her hands together with joy that her smart granddaughter grasped such a difficult concept.

Cosmic Kitty let out a deep sigh. That was a lot to understand. She would have to ask Mr. Tortoise about it when she was back in her realm. But for now, her curiosity kicked in once again.

CK decided to check out this new world before heading back. She turned to look around and really survey her surroundings, and for the first time, she noticed two small beings hovering slightly above her head. She had never noticed them before, and she jumped back with surprise upon seeing them, letting out a small yelp. The one to her left side smiled at her, in a sweet and knowing way. The one to her right gave her a stern look of disapproval, with arms crossed over his chest.

As she regained her composure, Cosmic Kitty asked: "Ummm... and you are?"

The one with arms crossed turned to speak to his counterpart. "Well, that's the thanks we get! She doesn't even know us! We have been looking after her and protecting her since before she was born--and all her previous lives as well! Isn't that a fine 'hello and thank you?'"

Turning back to Cosmic Kitty, he continued, "And now you go getting yourself caught in a portal, so I have to protect you not just from your own world, but other worlds as well! No respect...Noooo respect."

CK looked closer at this being, now hovering at her right shoulder. He was about 6 inches in height. He had large ears similar to a seahorse in depth but shaped more like elephant ears, and with the attitude of a military officer, though CK had no reference for this because there was no military in her dimension. His body seemed quite fluid and formless, almost like a jellyfish she once met. As he ranted about her escapades, his body contracted, coming together and then moving apart again, pushing him up and down in the air. It was almost as if he were a large blossom opening upside down when he was letting in air. Then, when he pulled his sides close together, he was pushing himself up in the air. His body shape reminded CK of a clove of garlic! She almost laughed at the thought of him being a clove of garlic with big elephant ears but held it in so as not to offend him directly.

With arms crossed and his tentacle-like "foot" tapping, he asked, "So – what do you have to say for yourself?"

CK looked at him with a blank stare. Thankfully, his partner came to her rescue.

"Don't worry about him, CK. His job is to keep you out of trouble. He is your Protector Guide," said the other being of light hovering around CK's shoulders.

CK took a good look at her. She was also approximately 6 inches tall, with a kind face and very wise eyes. She was a pink being, also heart-shaped like CK, with whiskers. Instead of hair and arms and legs, though, she had spirals of energetic cords coming out where arms and hair might be. She also had a long cord at the base of her body, curled up to stay out of the way. These cords were used to connect with CK when needed, providing her with downloads of information and knowledge to help with her life journey.

The pink heart being continued, "I am your Life Guide. My job is to help you gather the wisdom and knowledge you need to make good decisions to keep you moving along your life purpose. Before you were born, we worked with you and the Council of Elders to determine what your soul needed to work on at this time. What did you need to learn and what lessons are you still struggling to experience? You see, your life on this planet is an opportunity for your soul to get to know itself better and show and express higher levels of development and understanding. That is your main reason for being here. It is also to help others in their development. We all work together for the good of everyone to help all souls find their purpose and develop further. Your Protector Guide and I have been with you for many, many lives. You have come a very long way since we first started working with your young soul thousands and thousands of years ago! We have always been there with you when you are 'in-body.' And when you do not have a body, we work with you in spirit. We are your spirit guides."

"Wow," was all CK could say.

But in her heart, she knew these beings. She had felt their presence many times before. She knew they were there. A hand that kept her from falling down a cliff while playing. A soft voice reminding her to be nice and thank her friends for their support. The tug of guidance and intuition that would recommend she take a specific path, read a specific book or even remind her to brush her teeth before bed. She knew. These were HER spirit guides!

"What should I call you?" CK asked.

Her protector guide spoke up. "I cannot tell you my name because it will cause me to lose some of my power to protect you. And YOU need protection! So you can just make up a nickname for me."

"Ok – how about Sam?" CK asked. The protector guide grimaced.

"We could call you John?" CK offered. Another odd look ensued.

Rolling her eyes above her head to think harder, CK said, "How about Sparky?"

The protector guide growled, "Absolutely Not! That sounds like a dog!"

"Ok….then how about Prog? "Pro" from "Protector" and "G" from "Guide"? said Cosmic Kitty. Prog was pleased with that solution.

"And you – what's your name?" said Cosmic Kitty, turning to her life guide.

"You can call me Celeste, short for Celestial because that is the kind of being I am," said the pink floating heart figure.

"Got it," said CK as she sat down on the rock once again to collect her wits.

The energy in this new place felt very heavy and dense. CK was finding it hard to breathe at times, especially when she was feeling anxious. She sat down in the grass and crossed her legs. It was time for some meditation. This was something she did as part of her daily ritual. She would spend an hour or more per day in meditation. She found it would relax and calm her mind and help her to connect with things that mattered. And this was definitely a time when she needed to relax and calm down!

As she sat in the grass, she could feel the cool vibration of the earth under her legs and back. But something was different. Mother Gaia didn't feel the same in this new world and Mother Gaia wasn't talking to her. Usually, in her meditation time, Cosmic Kitty would sit and breathe deeply. She would extend her energy down into the core of the planet, and the great being who looked after the planet would send energy back up to her in an exchange and connection that was both loving and rejuvenating. But this time, there was nothing. Her energetic grounding cord was having difficulty finding a place to anchor.

CK was determined to continue with her meditation. She sat still, closed her eyes and focused on her breath. Deep breath in. Hold it. Deep breath out. All the way. Deep breath in. Hold it. Deep breath out. All the way. After several deep breaths, she began to feel better.

CK checked in with her body, asking each part to relax and become quiet. She started with her feet and worked her way up to her head and face, finally fully relaxing into her meditation. Just as she was starting to feel a bit more centered and grounded, a large thud came from out of nowhere!

Startled, she opened her eyes. The ground beneath her shook and she could feel the trees around her crying out. She hadn't noticed it previously, but she could feel some of the energy of the other beings around her. The trees, the flowers and even some of the rocks gave off different kinds of energy. They cried out as several of them fell, pushed over at their roots by a large, angry-looking metal machine. Cosmic Kitty could not believe what she was seeing! Someone or something was purposely pulling the trees out of the ground and rolling over the flowers and other shrubs and greenery, as well! What was happening here?? This was madness!

Cosmic Kitty could feel the fear of all the little animals living in the trees running for their lives to get out of the way of the beast of a machine and to dodge the falling trees. She could sense their confusion at having their homes destroyed and their friends, the trees, knocked down. She started walking toward the metal beast to see if she could have a talk with it and explain that it was hurting those around it, and perhaps it might stop.

Prog grabbed her shoulder. "No, CK – it's not safe. Don't go over there. This is not the same as your world. You cannot politely ask them to stop and expect a good response."

"But they need to stop! These trees and flowers and animals are so scared and upset!" CK exclaimed.

"I know," replied Prog, "but not now. It is more important to keep you safe to continue your own journey than to try and change a world you don't live in."

"I have to try," said CK. "They need to stop!"

"No," replied Prog, "it's not safe because you don't live here."

"But what if I DID live here? Couldn't I stop it then?" implored CK.

"Perhaps," said Prog, "or at least you would be better equipped to try."

CK got an odd look on her face. Prog and Celeste could tell that she was thinking hard about the situation and also considering Prog's advice. Suddenly a look of inspiration came across CK's face, and she exploded with her idea.

"Then let's go find ME in THIS world! Cosmic Kitty from this world can stop this craziness from happening!" exclaimed CK.

Celeste and Prog looked at each other with raised eyebrows. Nana Whiskers had already wandered behind a rock when all the noise started. Even though it couldn't hurt her, she still hated loud noises.

Though it worried them, Celeste and Prog could not stop Cosmic Kitty. Free will is an element of the soul's evolution. Guides are here to help and protect, but they cannot force a soul to do anything the soul does not want to do. And souls can be very stubborn, even those living in the fifth dimension. Cosmic Kitty was no exception.

CK gathered herself up and set her intent. She knew that if she focused her intent on exactly what she wanted, she would be able to manifest it quickly. Within seconds of setting her intention to find herself in THIS dimension, a direction popped into her mind. "This way," she said to her spiritual posse, pointing in a westward direction. "Let's go find *me*." And off they went.

Chapter 3

WE ARE NOT IN JOY-VILLE ANYMORE

Cosmic Kitty walked off quickly, heading west towards the area that would be in the same spot as her village back in Joy-Ville. Nana Whiskers, Celeste, and Prog gave each other a look of concern, let out a big collective sigh and followed closely behind CK as she walked down the path to find herself in this world.

CK marched out of the forest, where she had been surrounded by trees, rocks, and some animals. She emerged out from the woods onto a "sidewalk," a path that followed beside the tree line. CK found that the third dimension was a strange place indeed! Not only was it barren of the wonderful hills, flowers, and animals from her home, but it also seemed to be full of this hard, rocky substance called "concrete." Block after block of gray, dull, lifeless cement. It was everywhere and on everything. It gave off no clear energy for CK. Most things, even rocks, give off some sort of vibration.

Back at home in Joy-Ville, CK loved to collect stones during her walks. Each one had a different vibration or frequency. She had been taught from an early age to use different stones to help subtly shift energy in the direction she wanted it to go. For example, Rose Quartz, a lovely pink stone, vibrated at the feeling of Love, while Black Obsidian, a heavy, dark stone, had a lower grounding vibration. Stones were even used to create harmony within the energy of Chakras, the energy points in the body. Her favorite healer friend, Lana, used them a lot. Of all the stones, CK's favorite was Larimar. It was a beautiful blue stone aligned to the throat Chakra. It helped her sing and helped those who heard her songs to understand their meaning more clearly.

But this cement had no strong vibration that CK could feel. She knew it had a frequency because everything does. But there seemed to be no helpful, healing vibrations coming from all the roads and sidewalks she was now encountering. CK thought that perhaps she just did not have the ability to connect with the cement because it was in the third dimension. She was certain it must have a lovely purpose and vibration, as everything does. Perhaps she just could not feel it yet, because it was too subtle.

As she walked along, CK found the sidewalk a bit tough to walk on as there were none of the natural cushions provided by the soil of her pathways at home. Her natural instincts and intuition told CK she needed to turn right onto the sidewalk to find the village where she lived in this dimension. She walked along the sidewalk for about a mile, walking uphill the whole way. Nana Whiskers floated behind CK and held her hands together tightly, trying not to tell CK what she should do. Celeste and Prog knew this was part of CK's journey to visit the third dimension; however, they were uncertain what decisions would come out of it from CK, as even the most perfect life blueprint still requires execution of free will by the soul that is experiencing it.

You see, each of us decides what we want to do with our life before we are born. We work with our Guides, Angels, God, and the Universe to determine what our path should be. We create our "Divine Blueprint." As part of our blueprint, we work with others in our Soul Group (other spirits who often live lifetimes with us as we help each other to grow) and create contracts with them. We agree to play a certain role in their life, and they play a certain role in our life. Sometimes we even agree to irritate each other, in the name of personal growth and experience. There are also souls who decide to live a life with physical disabilities, either to help others in their learning process or to work on their own learning. As spirits, we all have lessons we are working on and each time we live a new life, we have specific things we want to accomplish during that lifetime, so we have contracts to help each other. For example, a soul may be someone's child in this lifetime, but in another lifetime play the parent or spouse of that person. It's all a big, beautiful divine plan for the personal growth and advancement of our souls, brought to us by the Creator.

Celeste and Prog knew all of this, of course. They knew everything would work out exactly as it should and Cosmic Kitty would be provided the opportunities she needed for growth and learning. However, the daily duty of keeping her safe and providing her guidance still fell to them. It was a job they loved, as they loved her very much. They wanted only the best for CK, and like all of our Guides, they were determined to provide as much support and help as possible to keep her moving forward on her plan. They also knew, however, that free will can mean the plan can execute in many different ways, some choices being a bit tougher on the soul than others.

As CK walked up the hill on the sidewalk, she wondered how big the village would be. She wondered if they had little cottage style houses built in collaboration with Mother Earth to provide shelter. She also wondered how they prepared their food and if they played the same games. As she topped the hill, she could see the "village" below. CK's eyes shot wide open. She could not believe what she was seeing! She thought there was a lot of concrete near the forest, but now it was everywhere! Huge buildings shot up, reaching to the sky, even touching some low clouds. There were dozens of them! Below the larger buildings were shorter buildings of every shape and size! Different colored signs, lights, and sounds lit up the area. CK also noticed vehicles for transportation everywhere – called "cars." She remembered Mr. Tortoise had told her about cars in one of his stories. Where CK lived, the beings could easily think about where they wanted to go, and they would just appear there. It was called teleporting. They didn't need vehicles. If she wanted to visit a friend far away, CK could focus her intention on where she wanted to be, gather her energy and transfer it to that new location. "Cars" were not needed. It seemed in this new dimension, cars were still in use. And wow, were they loud and noisy!

The dull haze CK had seen when she first came through the portal was now much more dense and dark. It took the shine off everything. From behind the clouds, CK saw her friend Sunny.

"Hello, Sunny!" CK exclaimed. "How are you today?"

No answer came back.

"Sunny, did you hear me? I asked how you were," said CK. Again, no reply.

"He can't hear you, dear," reminded Nana Whiskers. "In this dimension, Sunny is just seen as a source of energy for providing light. He is not a friend, like in our world."

CK frowned. She missed her friends and was hoping for a big "Good Afternoon" from this one.

"Oh well," said CK, disappointed. "Let's keep moving. I feel that the other **me** is somewhere down in all that shiny hard stuff," she said, pointing to the city down the hill.

CK and her spiritual posse crossed over the top of the hill and headed down toward the city area. They dodged these things called "cars," incurring lots of noisy honking from many of the drivers. As they walked into the city, CK looked up at the big buildings around her. She had never seen such high structures. Only the mountains and hills were this big in her world. She wondered why they didn't just fall over.

"Mother Gaia must be providing pretty strong cords to hold them down!" said CK.

Celeste laughed. "CK – these are buildings made of concrete. Mother Gaia is not supporting them as she does in your world. They have used steel beams, a very hard substance, to hold them up. It is something the people in this world made themselves, digging out the materials from the minerals in the mountains," Celeste explained.

"But why would they do that?" asked CK. "Why would they dig up the minerals and destroy the mountains when they could just ask Mother Gaia to work with them and provide housing and structures?"

"Because this world does not yet have the same level of understanding and connection with their environment and the planet that we have in the fifth dimension," explained Celeste. "They are still fighting her – trying to do it their own way through dominating the planet instead of working with the planet. There are many people who are learning and working hard to help the others understand that dominance and destruction are not progress and that they don't have to destroy something to live comfortably. But the rest of the planet does not yet understand that message, though many are beginning to awaken to it," Celeste explained.

"Oh, I see," said CK. "Then what are these big structures used for?"

"People live in many of them, called apartments. Others are stores to buy things. Still, others hold businesses, which is how people work and make money," said Celeste.

"What's money?" asked CK.

"Money is how people in this dimension pay each other for things. That is how they pay for food, a place to live, clothes to wear, things for their homes--that sort of thing. It is a form of barter. Instead of just doing jobs that are natural for a person and using their gifts for everyone, here they use money to exchange for services, clothes, and food. It's just a different way of living compared with Joy-Ville."

"Sounds very complicated," CK said with a confused look. "I don't understand why they don't just share what is needed with everyone. In our world, Mr. Tortoise is a teacher because it's his passion. Lois Lamb loves to make clothes, so everyone always has something to wear. Actually, she makes too much sometimes! Hoya has a fabulous garden, and we all help pick things to eat and share and even cook together. I like to sing so I entertain our friends whenever they want to hear a tune. Everyone does what they are good at and what they like to do. Some people even love to clean! That would not be me. But Boppy is amazing with a mop! She loves to see a messy floor shine!"

Celeste gave a sigh. "I know," she said. "But these folks are not there yet. In time, hopefully, they will figure out that life does not have to be a struggle. The lower dimensions still don't understand how working in harmony with each other, and the planet can lead to longer and more easy lives. Here, they only live to be 70-80 years old! Life is hard. It's hard on the body, the spirit and the mind. They work very hard and put a lot of toxic substances into their bodies. No wonder they die very tired!"

"That's sad," said CK.

"It is," said Celeste. "But always remember that is part of their journey. This is a reality that part of you is living in as well. And part of you is here in the third dimension to help your soul grow and learn lessons, just like the You who lives in Joy-Ville."

"I think I understand," said CK, and she continued to walk along the sidewalks under the big steel structures in search of *Herself*.

This is not a very happy place, thought CK. *Let's get that tree monster stopped and get back home.*

Chapter 4

THE SCHOOL YARD

As the group continued to walk along the city streets, Nana Whiskers finally asked, "CK, where are we going?"

"I am not completely certain," replied CK, "but I feel like we are heading in the right direction."

CK had learned years ago to use her intuition. She had spent hours of time in meditation and prayer listening to her heart and understanding what her intuition (and her Guides, though she did not know it at the time) was saying to her. Because she had become so good at listening to herself, she was able to pick up on the vibration of the part of her that was here, but not with her currently. CK led the group through back alleys, across busy streets and even through a few stores. She felt certain the "*other me*" had been in these stores, perhaps shopping for clothes or other items.

Finally, CK walked out of a store and got a "hit" that her third dimension self was nearby. She walked a few more blocks, and there, in front of a school building, she saw an image of herself. The girl she was looking at did not look that much like CK, though she had a few of the same characteristics. Her cheekbones were similar, and her hair was wavy, but it had been straightened with an iron. She had a slight "heart" shape to her face, but nothing like CK's face. She wore a pink sleeveless dress with large rectangular patterns on it. She was a bit heavier than CK and slightly taller. She was standing in a group with two other girls, wearing similar outfits.

CK got closer and heard them talking.

"What are we going to do this weekend, Katherine?" one of the girls asked CK's third dimension self.

Ah – Katherine! Thought CK. *That is my name in this dimension. Cool!*

"Not sure," replied Katherine. "Rick is having a party at his house. There is also a new band playing at Queenies we could go see."

"Queenies is boring," the girl replied. "There is just nothing to do around here at all."

CK got very excited about seeing herself. She barged right into the schoolyard to have a conversation before her Spirit Guides and Nana Whiskers could stop her.

"Hi Katherine," CK began breathlessly.

"What do YOU want and how do you know my name?" snarled Katherine with an exaggerated tone of irritation.

CK was taken aback by the harshness of herself, but she was not deterred.

"I am Cosmic Kitty, and I am you from the fifth dimension. I came here via a portal while walking through the woods at home. I came to this strange village to find you because you see, there is a metal monster killing all the trees and animals back in the forest, and I need your help to stop it," CK quickly spouted out.

Katherine and her two friends stared at Cosmic Kitty with a look of both confusion and disgust. And then they did something very odd… they laughed.

"Did Rick put you up to this? I bet he made that story up himself," Katherine said.

"No," said CK, "I don't know anyone called 'Rick.' I am you, just from a different place."

Katherine scowled, and a slightly ruthless look passed over her eyes very briefly. "Look, weirdo – I don't know who you are or where you come from, but where do you get off calling yourself me?" Katherine snapped.

CK shrank down, taken aback by the harsh tone and words. No one had ever spoken to her like that. It just wasn't done. Unable to decide what to say next, CK mumbled an excuse and quickly walked away.

Katherine screamed behind her, "Get out of here, you freak! We don't need your kind here making up stories and bringing your whiskers and curly hair into our schoolyard!"

The tears began to stream down CK's freckled, pale cheeks. She couldn't believe someone, especially herself, could be so mean! Her heart sank as she realized what had just happened. She found an alley between two buildings and sank down to cry. Celeste, Prog, and Nana Whiskers tried to console her, but she didn't want to hear it. Her heart hurt in a way she had never experienced.

"Why do they have to be so mean?" she asked no one in particular. "I didn't do anything to them. I just wanted to introduce myself and get some help," CK said between sobs.

Celeste and Nana Whiskers hovered close by CK, letting her cry out her emotional hurt, while Prog stood guard to watch for other encounters with people from this land.

After an hour of riding her emotions and letting them out (something CK learned as a child), she began to feel a little better. The tears were cleansing, though she still felt a dull ache in her heart where the words from Katherine stung. Her heart was shining a little less brightly now as she spent more time in the third dimension and encountered an environment and people with a lower vibration.

"Come on, CK," said Prog. "Let's get back to the portal and get you home safely."

"No," said CK. "I still have a job to do here. I need to get 'me' to stop that metal monster."

"But CK, you have already tried, and all you got for it were harsh words from a bully," Nana Whiskers pointed out.

"I know," said CK, "but I just can't believe this is her true nature. I want to talk to her again and see if I can engage her 'higher self' instead of the 'lower self' I met today."

"I'm not sure that's a good idea, CK. Sometimes our worst and most fierce enemy is often ourselves, even when we live in the same dimension, much less a different one," offered Celeste.

"I know," said CK, "but I have to try."

Prog, Celeste, and Nana Whiskers let out another big collective sigh. It was going to be a long day.

Chapter 5

UNDERSTANDING KATHERINE

Cosmic Kitty decided to pull herself together in this new land. She decided she needed to center herself for a few moments. Taking several deep breaths, CK pulled together her strength to get up from the ground. The alley was not the best place for her to hang out, she decided. A plan was needed if she wanted to stop the metal monster and get back home again. And a plan she must decide.

As she rose, CK looked around for Prog, Celeste, and Nana Whiskers. She found she could not see them very well. Their color was not as crisp as it had been and she could see the brick wall on the other side of them as if they were transparent and faded into it.

Concerned, CK asked Celeste, "Why are you so light? I can see the wall right through you now."

With a knowing look, Celeste explained that the longer CK stayed in the third dimension, the more her vibration would also drop to match the world she was in. The lower CK's vibration went, the harder it would be for her to hear and see her spirit guides and Nana Whiskers, at least physically.

"Your vibration is going down, CK, because of the world around you. That means it will be harder to see us as well, just like Katherine in this world cannot see us," explained Celeste.

This concerned CK, of course, as she was used to having her spiritual companions around. However, CK decided that she still needed to resolve this issue with the metal beast and THEN they would make their way back to Joy-Ville.

"Think, think, think," CK said to herself. "How can I get Katherine to believe me and help with this metal monster?"

"Perhaps try feel, feel, feel," came the soft voice of Nana Whiskers.

"Hmm..." said CK, "interesting concept."

This guidance and recommendation made sense to CK. She knew that the root of most problems, and often their solutions, came from feelings and emotions, versus using only logical thinking. She had been taught by Mr. Tortoise and others in Joy-Ville long ago that all emotions come from one of two places. They either come from Love or Fear. And actually, even Fear usually has much deeper roots in Love. In Joy-Ville, there is very little fear. As a result, there is very little anger, hatred, or even frustration. That is why they also have no violence or even competition. There is no need for it because much of the fear is gone from their society. However, in this third dimension, it was very clear to CK that fear still existed. Even just walking down the road, she was afraid of being struck by one of those "car things" people were using for transportation. CK did not feel safe in this place, which meant there was fear for those who lived here as well.

"I wonder how Katherine feels?" CK asked herself and anyone who could answer. "I wonder why she was so mean to me – what was she afraid of that made her react that way?"

Prog piped in. "This whole place!" he said. "It's not safe. You can get hurt because no one is watching out for each other. People do not openly share love. There is competition for money, competition for friends. They believe there is not enough for everyone, and they are AFRAID of missing out."

"Not having enough what?" asked CK with a confused look on her face, as this had never been her experience in Joy-Ville.

"Not enough food, homes, friends, money, clothes, cars, fame....you name it--they think there is not enough to go around," explained Prog, now beginning to dim further as he hovered above her shoulder.

"But most of all, and most importantly, they don't think there is enough LOVE to go around," chimed in Celeste. "And that is the worst part. So they do things to try and get people to like and love them. In the place where you saw Katherine, they call this 'popularity' or being in the 'popular crowd.' The kids will do things that they think will make others like them more."

"That's crazy!" exclaimed CK. "Of course there is more than enough love to go around. And you don't like or love people because of money, clothes or friends. You love them because each person is unique and beautiful and part of the Divine Creator. We all have pure light in our soul if we will use it. The rest doesn't matter."

Celeste went on, "**I** know that, and **you** know that, but the beings in this dimension are only starting to understand that concept. Some of them get it and agree with you. Many others do not understand it and live with the fear that they are not enough. So they are constantly doing things or buying things to make other people like them. Of course, it doesn't work unless the people they are trying to attract also believe these things matter. So it's a vicious circle of trying to impress each other, all the while living in fear that someone will figure out they are not good enough."

CK looked down, and a tear rolled down her cheek. All of this information was distressing and made her feel upset for the beings that lived in this dimension, especially for Katherine, who seemed to be caught in this trap. The more time she spent in the third dimension of her world, the more she could feel the pain coming from the other part of herself who lived here full time.

"That's a very sad way to live. How can you ever feel real joy or real connection or compassion if you are worried about getting other people to like you? Don't they realize that we are all 'enough' just as we are and the most important validation and approval come from ourselves, not from those around us?" asked CK.

"Many folks here do not have that understanding, including Katherine," Celeste continued. "But do not judge them for it. This is their journey. They must come to their own understanding of what truly matters in this world and that they really don't need anything or anyone to prove they are worthy. It all comes from inside, and they will realize this in their own good time, in this lifetime or the next one."

As CK thought about herself who lived here and began to feel the emotions of Katherine, her heart felt very tight, and she had trouble breathing. Her heart Chakra, or energy, felt like it was closing up like a fist, getting tighter and tighter. Then something very odd happened. CK got a strange vision in her head. It was located just at her third eye, the energy center in the middle of the forehead that connects with things we cannot always see with our physical eyes. Often these things are in another dimension or may be visions of the past or the future. CK could see, clear as day, Katherine in her home. It was an average house as these things go. It had two bedrooms and a shared bathroom. The kitchen and living room were pretty typical, with tables, chairs and a few sofas for the family and guests to relax. A big screen TV hung on the wall, obviously the most expensive "furniture" in the house. Katherine was sitting on the couch watching some strange show where the people seemed to be arguing quite a lot.

Katherine's mother and father were also in CK's vision. They were loud and noisy. Katherine seemed to be ignoring them, but the pained look on her face made it clear she heard and felt every cruel word they spoke to each other. CK was not exactly sure what they were yelling about, but it didn't matter as the tone made it clear it was not a good topic. Then, they turned on Katherine. They yelled at her to get up and do something productive. They called her "worthless" and other equally degrading things. Katherine just sat there and took it, pretending to ignore her parents as tears streamed down her cheeks.

Cosmic Kitty couldn't stand it anymore. She opened her eyes wide and shook her head to get the vision to go away. Watching this verbal fighting and abuse was more than she could stand to see or feel.

Poor Katherine! What a terrible way to live! thought CK. *No wonder she was mean to me. She doesn't know how else to act. She is not getting any love at home, so she is trying to find it with her friends and trying to get them to love her by acting superior to others.* It all became clear to CK very quickly. It was obvious that Katherine did not feel worthy herself. So she thought to put down others would make her feel better about herself. If someone else could be lower than her, she might be able to get love from other people, like her friends. It was all so sad! CK was no longer upset with Katherine; she now felt great compassion and love for her. She was not angry or hurt but felt sorry for her. It was obvious Katherine was living in fear--fear of conditional love based on her actions and whether she "did something productive" or not. There was fear of not having friends. They might turn on her just like her parents did. And having someone like Cosmic Kitty show up and talk about weird places and odd things did not help the situation if she were already feeling so insecure. CK got it. She now understood. But now she had to decide what to do about it. How could she get through to Katherine? How would this new knowledge help her get Katherine to help with the metal beast? CK knew she could now find a way!

Chapter 6

BACK TO THE SCHOOLYARD

With great and renewed confidence, Cosmic Kitty decided to return to the schoolyard to see if Katherine was around. She was not yet sure what she was going to do or say, but she knew she would figure it out when she got there.

CK approached the yard, and Katherine was still there. Obviously, school had now finished for the day, but Katherine did not seem to be in any hurry to get home. CK could certainly understand why. Katherine sat by herself on a bench watching as some younger kids played on the swings nearby. Her book bag sat crumpled up beside her, obviously unused. She didn't seem to have many books in there for homework that day. Her face was drawn into a slight frown, though all CK could see was the sadness in her eyes.

"What do you want?" Katherine asked sharply as CK approached her.

"Nothing really," said CK. "I just wanted to talk. You seemed lonely just sitting here so I thought you could use some company. I am new in this village, so I am lonely too."

Katherine raised an eyebrow at CK, shifting her head up slightly to look up at her.

What a strange-looking girl! Her head has such an odd heart shape, and she really could use some help with those long hairs, Katherine thought, referring to CKs whiskers. But since no one was around and her friends had gone home, Katherine didn't make a big deal about CK sitting down on the bench beside her.

"So what do you do here?" asked CK in a polite manner.

Katherine looked up in disbelief. *Really? She doesn't know? That's weird,* thought Katherine.

"This is where I go to school," said Katherine in a cool, crisp tone.

"Oh neat! That's great! I love to learn about new places and how things work and how to do stuff! How wonderful--what a fabulous place this must be!" exclaimed CK.

"Yeah, it's great," Katherine returned with a dry, sarcastic tone that made it clear she thought it was anything but. "We learn stuff no one ever uses, and then we take tests ....it's super," Katherine continued sarcastically.

Cosmic Kitty did not completely understand sarcasm, but she could feel in her heart that Katherine was not speaking her truth.

"You don't really believe it's super, do you?" CK asked, drawing on her intuition for the real story.

"Of course not," Katherine shot back. "What planet did YOU come from? We just go to school and learn stuff that doesn't matter. Then we get a job to pay bills. We marry someone we fight with for years. Maybe have a few kids and then we die. That's how it works. What's there to be happy about?"

CK was taken aback. She had never heard someone describe their life in such an unhappy way...past, present or future. Most people in Joy-Ville were not only content, but happy as well.

CK quickly scanned her mind in search of a reply to Katherine's question. She thought quickly about what made HER happy when she was in Joy-Ville.

"Well actually, I am quite happy. Where I live, the people are very nice to each other. We are respectful and kind. There is plenty of Love to go around for everyone. We work together doing jobs we enjoy and share in the work. We even have a good relationship with nature," explained CK.

"You ARE from another planet!" exclaimed Katherine.

CK just smiled a knowing smile and did not respond. She felt that would be too much information to share with Katherine in this world. More information about the fifth dimension and Joy-Ville might not be a good idea given the previous reaction to this information.

CK decided to change the subject. "Can I ask you a question?" CK pondered.

Katherine just looked at her, but she did not say 'no'. For some reason, this strange girl, from what must be some foreign country, seemed to be growing on Katherine. She didn't know why, but just sharing a bench and sharing the same space with this odd girl made her feel a little nice inside. The fist in Katherine's heart seemed to be opening slightly, or at least loosening up on its death grip. What Katherine did not know was that while CK was sitting next to her, she was visualizing Katherine surrounded by white and gold light. She pictured that light of pure love and joy surrounding Katherine and streaming down through her body. Obviously, Katherine could feel some of its energy and feel some of her connection to CK as well.

Since Katherine did not say 'no,' CK continued.

"Why were you so mean to me earlier today?" asked CK, and stopped. She didn't want to add more to the question, though she felt like she knew the answer.

Katherine paused. Normally she would have answered this question with additional insults and shouting at the person who asked it. That's what her parents always did. Katherine had learned two ways to respond to difficult questions and discussions. At school, she would use violence and raise her voice in a defensive way. However, at home she would go to silence and just shut down, not responding at all. But now she felt odd, different. She didn't want to scream at CK. A small voice in her head (probably the influence of Celeste in this dimension) told her she could trust CK and it was safe to have a real conversation with her. She could drop some of her defenses. This girl was from out of town anyway, so it didn't really matter what she said. No one would care.

Katherine finally decided on an answer. "Because you were embarrassing me," she said. "You were talking about weird things and saying you were me and knew me. I didn't want anyone to think I knew you."

"Oh," replied CK. "I'm very sorry. I did not mean to embarrass you. That was not my intent. Please forgive me. I only wanted to get some help with a serious problem out in the woods, and I thought you could help me." CK took a breath and paused, letting her words sink in. Katherine did not reply, and silence filled the space between the two girls.

Cautiously, CK posed another question. "I'm curious. Why do you care if people think you know me?" CK slowly asked.

Katherine thought about this question for a moment. It was actually a good question and one she had never considered. Why DID she care so much? What made her decide she needed to yell at this girl she didn't even know? She sounded like her parents when she did that. This last thought made Katherine cringe. But again the original question popped in – *why do you care what people think?* As Katherine thought about this question, a large wave of emotion came from deep inside her and her eyes filled with tears. It was obvious this question had hit a nerve for her. When the answer finally came out, Katherine could barely whisper it.

"Because I don't want to be alone, and if they think I am weird too, people won't want to be around me," she whispered in a low voice. "I am afraid of having no friends since they are all I have."

Cosmic Kitty just nodded her head to show Katherine that she understood what she was saying.

"It's tough to live in a place like this, it seems, where there is so much negativity. Friends would be good to help us through it," CK empathized, desperately trying to understand and show compassion for Katherine.

Katherine just said, "Yep" and went quiet again.

Cautiously CK began again. "I'm very lucky. I have good friends back home, and they love me no matter what I do. I can act silly or crazy or even disappear on adventures, and they have to find me, but they always love me regardless. I never have to impress them or do things to make them like me. We love each other unconditionally because we understand that we are each beautiful and unique in our own way. We don't want to all be alike – that's boring!" CK explained. "And that's what good friends are like. When we find those people we connect with, those people who are truly our family, whether we are related to them or not, those people who accept us exactly as we are and love us for who we are…those are our true friends. Those friends are the ones who support us when we are happy or sad and who help us grow and develop, and we help them to grow and develop too. I call them my 'puddle friends' because they will jump into puddles and splash water with me, just because I want to. When you find those friends, you can be yourself. But in the end, the only thing that matters is whether or not you love yourself. Loving and accepting yourself just as you are is the most important thing of all!"

Katherine quietly listened to Cosmic Kitty as she continued to describe what true friends are like. CK told Katherine a little bit about her friends in the fifth dimension, though not in great detail, so as not to freak Katherine out too much. Katherine took it all in, wondering if she would ever be able to find her true friends. At that moment, Katherine also decided that she didn't need to do things to make other people like her. She needed to spend more time and energy just to be herself, whatever that looked like. It was a good realization for Katherine and made her feel happy inside. For the first time in years, she felt a warm glow as her heart began to loosen and open up more to joy. It was a wonderful first step for her.

Finally, Katherine did something very unusual. She apologized to Cosmic Kitty for the mean things she had said earlier. And oddly enough, after saying she was sorry, Katherine felt great! The weight of the world felt like it had come off her shoulders. The air around her cleared and became lighter. And she was surprised by how much better she felt!

After the girls had sat talking for an hour on the bench, the sun began to set. Katherine said she had to go home. CK looked up at the sun setting and realized just how much she missed her own home as well. Sunny would be just going down behind the hills, sending out his last few rays. Moon Man would be starting his early preparation for ascending into the sky, along with CK's good friend Starlight. Oh how much CK missed Joy-Ville! And she also found in all the excitement that she was hungry as well! She hadn't eaten for hours.

Katherine looked at CK, who was gazing off into the distance, thinking about her home.

"Are you going home now?" Katherine asked CK.

CK thought for a moment and decided to be honest. "Actually no, I can't leave yet. I guess I'll just sleep here tonight. It's a beautiful night, and I'm sure I will rest well."

"WHAT?!?" Katherine almost screamed. "You can't stay here! It's not safe at night. Strange people come around, and it's dark!"

"I'm sure it's fine," said CK. "It's a lovely place to hang out."

"No – you cannot stay here," said Katherine. "Come home with me. You can sleep in my room tonight and go back home tomorrow. Have you eaten anything? I have food as well."

Cosmic Kitty was not sure what to do. She looked around to ask her guides and Nana Whiskers for their thoughts, only to realize that she could no longer hear or see them! *Oh no,* thought CK, *I have lost my guides!* Then she remembered they were not lost, only at a different vibration, making it hard to find them. In her heart, CK knew they were still around. She just would have to work harder to get their messages.

After considering Katherine's offer, CK decided that the part of her that lived in this world probably had a much better idea of what was needed to be safe here. So Cosmic Kitty agreed to go home with Katherine for the night.

Chapter 7

A NIGHT IN JOY-LESS

The two girls walked side by side over several blocks through the city streets. Cosmic Kitty was still amazed at the amount of concrete and glass she saw everywhere. There were very few trees around. She saw some bushes and flowers planted in little boxes without much room to grow. There were no animals to speak of – only blocks and blocks of this hard gray and white substance. Even looking up, all she could see were just floors and floors of little windows and small railings where evidently the people in this land lived. She could no longer see her friend Sunny, though he had not been very friendly in this particular dimension. He had gone behind a building, and all she could see were long shadows of huge buildings covering up the last remaining sunlight of the day.

As the girls walked along, Cosmic Kitty asked Katherine, "Do you like living here? I mean in this village with all the cement and glass and no trees?"

Katherine shrugged her shoulders. "It's ok, I guess. I don't love it or hate it. It's just where I live. I have never really known much else. This city is where I grew up," she offered.

"Don't you miss the trees and animals?" asked CK inquisitively.

"Not really," replied Katherine. "They were never really around growing up. We did have a bird once, though. It was lovely. It would sing and chirp. It loved to eat sunflower seeds and splash in the water bowl in its cage."

"Its' cage!?!" exclaimed CK. "You kept it locked up??"

"Of course," replied Katherine. "Otherwise it would fly around the house and poop all over the sofa and floor, or it would fly out the window and get away."

CK decided not to reply. She was in shock. She had to take several deep breaths to regain her composure and not let Katherine see how upset she was with the idea of putting a bird in a cage. How could they want to keep anything as lovely as a bird locked up? Birds should be free to come and go as they please. They can visit when they feel like it, but it's not right to cage any animal, especially one that likes to spread its wings and fly into the sky and trees. That's just cruel. CK made a mental note to ask Mr. Tortoise about this. She didn't understand it at all, but she didn't want to make Katherine mad by asking her why she would do such a mean thing. Obviously, it seemed to be normal in this dimension.

After getting over the shock, CK caught her breath again. This time she took a different avenue and decided to ask Katherine about the metal monster.

"I saw all these birds and other animals in the woods today, and they were very upset," CK began. "They were running away and quite frightened. The trees and flowers were being pushed over by this big metal beast. I don't know what you call it, but it was quite scary and very destructive!"

"Oh – that's a bulldozer," Katherine explained. "If it's the woods by that hill that looks like a whale, they are clearing those woods to make a shopping mall."

"What's a 'shopping mall'?" asked CK.

"Really??" said Katherine. "You don't know what a mall is? Where did you say you were from? Obviously, somewhere very remote if you don't have shopping malls." Thankfully Katherine continued her explanation before CK had to answer the question of where she was from.

"A shopping mall is a big building where a bunch of stores sell different stuff people want to buy. Usually, there are a lot of clothing stores there, but they also have electronics, books, shoes, makeup, sports equipment, sunglasses…all sorts of things. They usually have some restaurants to buy food and even some places to get your nails and hair done."

"Wow," said CK. "That sounds like a big place for everyone to go and share. We have something like that too, but much smaller. Everyone just goes and gets what they need and brings what they have made to share with others."

Katherine laughed. "That sounds very quaint," she said, "but at the shopping mall, you need money to buy things. No one is sharing or swapping things they have made. Big companies have produced the clothes and food and other items. So we all work (or our parents work) to make money to buy these things. Sometimes we even work for the companies that produce them."

CK thought that sounded very odd. But she decided not to say so.

The girls finally arrived at Katherine's house. It was a small house, squeezed between two other small houses, with a tiny yard and more concrete for the driveway. Thankfully, no one was there, so Katherine did not have to explain why she brought this strange girl from a foreign country home with her.

"My parents often stay out very late, usually in different places," explained Katherine. "Let's get something to eat."

Katherine and CK walked into the little kitchen area. It was splashed full of beige and brown and these funky, shiny plastic floors. The kitchen reminded CK of the hazy environment of this entire dimension. Katherine opened the door of a large box-shaped container. A blast of cold air came out. She retrieved a brightly colored box from the freezer, covered in red, yellow and blue markings. It had a picture of something round on the top and the words "Pizza" spelled out on the box.

Wonderful! CK thought. *This should be super food. Look how colorful it is. It must be very ripe and good indeed.*

"Why don't you sit down on the couch while I fix us some pizza," Katherine said. "How about a Coke to drink?"

"Anything is great," said CK, who was now starving.

Katherine took the frozen pizza from its package and put it into a small metal box on the counter. Then she hit a few buttons on the box to turn it on. It made a loud humming noise. CK watched her curiously. While most of the food consumed in Joy-Ville was usually eaten in its natural state from the Earth, they did have stoves and ways to cook food. However, CK had never seen a contraption like this. The box continued to hum, and she could see a light inside as the pizza turned around on a glass plate. Meanwhile, Katherine pulled out two brightly colored red metal cans from the other side of the large cold box and handed one to CK. CK just looked at it. She didn't know what it was or what to do with it, so she watched Katherine.

Katherine pulled a little ring off the top of the can, and it created an opening in the top to get inside the can. Then she put the can to her lips and began to slurp down the substance inside with great pleasure and speed. Cosmic Kitty closely examined her can, trying to figure out how to copy what Katherine had done. She pulled off the top of the can and created the opening just as Katherine had. Cautiously CK put the can to her lips and took a small sip.

Yuck! She thought. *That's disgusting!* The sickly sweet syrup burned her throat and lips with spicy, tingling liquid. Thankfully, the drink was cold, or it would have burned her throat even more.

How can she drink this stuff!?! thought CK. But she didn't want to insult her host, so she said nothing and just smiled. She took one more very small sip before putting the can down, just to be polite.

"I don't suppose you have any water as well," CK asked as nicely as she could muster while her lips were still burning from the brown substance.

"Sure," said Katherine, and pulled a glass out of the cabinet and filled it with water from the kitchen sink. CK had learned long ago that she should speak up for what she needed from others, but in a way that did not disrespect their personal choices. To ask for something different is perfectly fine, though it's important not to judge someone if they make a different choice.

CK was grateful for the water. Though it tasted very funny and had an odd flavor, it was definitely a better choice than the red can.

From out of nowhere a loud "ding!" caused CK to nearly jump out of her skin. "What was that!?!" she screamed.

Katherine laughed while also looking at CK in disbelief. "Uh…the microwave," she said. "Dinner's ready." Katherine couldn't believe CK had never seen a microwave. How could someone live without one in this day and age? *Oh CK,* Katherine thought. *She must come from a developing country if they don't even have microwaves. How sad.* A feeling of compassion and warmth passed over her heart, loosening the fist just a little bit more, even if it was misdirected.

Katherine pulled the pizza from the microwave and, using a large knife, cut it into slices and put it on two plates. She handed CK a plate and the girls sat down on the couch to eat.

CK watched Katherine closely to see HOW she would eat these interesting triangles of food. Katherine picked up a piece and started at the smallest end, taking bites until the whole slice was gone. CK took a deep breath, said a quiet prayer thanking the food for giving up its life for her nourishment, and took a bite. She chewed and chewed and chewed some more. CK had learned to chew her food well, appreciating each bite. But this was different. The food formed a dough-like paste in her mouth as she chewed it. She could taste tomatoes and onions and peppers and garlic (some of her favorite foods). But the white crust and melted topping were both a bit confusing. In her land, they didn't make cheese from the milk of animals nor did they grow wheat for flour. Everything was harvested in a more natural way, straight from the ground or trees on which it grew. She didn't mind this funny texture, as she was always willing to try new things. She was curious as to what these white parts of the meal were, but decided not to ask. Katherine was obviously enjoying her food, quickly eating her slices of the pizza. Cosmic Kitty slowly ate two pieces of pizza, considering the taste and texture carefully. She wanted to remember how it felt in her mouth so she could explain it to her friends back home and ask Mr. Tortoise about the white stuff on top.

When dinner was finished, the two girls sat on the couch. Katherine turned on the television. It was the same loud, noisy show that CK had seen in her vision. The people were saying mean things to each other and then talking to someone separately to tell them how they felt about the mean things they said to someone else. CK was very confused by the show. They had a form of entertainment in Joy-Ville, but it was never like this.

"What kind of show is this?" CK asked Katherine.

"Oh – it's a new reality TV show," responded Katherine casually. "The point is that these people are trying to live in a house together, but they chose people who wouldn't get along very well. They put them into teams and get them to compete for money. But sometimes they also put in distractions or give unfair tools to one side to help them win to see how everyone will react."

"That sounds terrible," said CK. "Why would they do that?"

"For the money and even to be famous," replied Katherine. "Even if you are bad or mean, you can be famous and make a lot of money, so people will try using these reality TV shows for that purpose."

"But why do people watch these shows?" asked CK

Katherine stopped suddenly. *What a good question,* she thought. She had to consider it for a moment. *Why DO we watch this junk? We all say it's junk, but we watch it anyway.* Katherine thought about this question for a few more minutes before an answer finally popped into her head, seemingly from nowhere (thank you, Celeste).

"Because if you see someone else's life and it's worse than yours, it makes you feel better about your own life and how hard it can be. It's also a distraction, and honestly, just something to do before bed."

Katherine was surprised by her answer. She had never thought about TV that way, and she certainly had never compared it to her own life. Perplexed, Katherine sat with this thought for a few more minutes. Where did it come from and was it true? Did she really only watch these shows because they were worse than her life? Did they make her feel better? Actually, no. She decided they did not make her feel better. In reality, they made her feel more depressed and more hopeless. What an interesting thought. She had never even considered that these shows were negative. Perhaps these shows were similar to why she would put people down at school and say mean things. Seeing someone else's life as worse than her own or putting someone else down to feel a little more superior were both very similar things. She wanted to feel better and so seeing a show about a family or household who was struggling or making someone else feel bad might just do that. But at that moment, Katherine realized that neither watching negative shows nor putting other people down would change how she felt about herself or her own life. Seeing others worse off did not make her position any better. Katherine's head and heart reeled with these new insights and information. It was so much to consider it actually made her dizzy to think about it.

CK could see the struggle on Katherine's face as she thought through these questions. She could also feel the tight fist in Katherine's heart starting to open up just a little bit more as she contemplated the answers.

"You look a little perplexed," said CK softly to her hostess.

"Just thinking…" replied Katherine, still off in a distant place.

"Ya know, when I am thinking about something important, I find it very useful to write down what I'm thinking in a journal. Then I can come back to it later if I want to think about it some more," offered CK.

"Hmm…good idea," Katherine mumbled as she continued to ponder the question of why she watched these shows and even further, why she put people down.

After a few minutes, Katherine got up and went to her school bag. She got out a piece of paper and started to write some thoughts on it.

Excellent! Thought CK. *This will be great for her!*

In the meantime, while Katherine was writing down some thoughts and grappling with her inner spirit, CK decided to see if she could find and connect with her own spiritual posse. She sat down in a big chair and crossed her legs. With a perfectly straight spine, CK sat up. She closed her eyes, put her hands in her lap facing upward and began to meditate. She could feel a vibration of love around her, obviously coming from her spirit guides and Nana Whiskers. But she still couldn't see them, even with her eyes closed. She also could not hear them, at least not directly. CK let out a big sigh. She was very frustrated at being alone in this strange world without direct communication with her guides. She didn't know them physically before she arrived in this land, but now she really wanted them to appear again.

After a few minutes of trying to reach them, CK gave up. She also realized she was very tired. It had been a long day, and that white dough pizza was sitting heavy in her stomach. CK asked Katherine where she could lie down to sleep. Just as Katherine was about to answer, the front door swung open with a bang.

"Hi, Honey! I'm hooomme," said a loud, slurring voice. "It's your daaaddddyyyyooo."

"Oh crud!" said Katherine. "My dad is home…and he's been drinking again," she added with an embarrassed side note.

CK wasn't sure what "drinking" meant in this world, but she was pretty sure it wasn't good, given Katherine's reaction.

CK and Katherine quickly went up the stairs to Katherine's room. Below them, they could hear the large man shouting at the counters when he bumped into them. A few minutes later, the door opened again. This time, they heard a woman's voice.

"What on earth have you been doing, George!?!" the woman asked. It was Katherine's mother. "You smell like a liquor store!"

Katherine's father had lost his job recently and taken to spending time with friends going to bars at night. He called it "networking." Katherine's mother, Celia, often worked late in her office. If she didn't leave by a certain time each day, she would sit in traffic for hours trying to drive home. Today was one of those days. With both of them usually out in the evenings, this left Katherine home alone more evenings than she could count. Even when her dad was working, he was usually home pretty late as well. On this particular evening, both her mother and father had come home around the same time. That was very unusual.

Katherine's mother continued, "George, why can't you be a normal father? You are always out with your friends, and you never help me around the house! You are useless as a husband!"

Katherine's father replied, "Well if you didn't nag me all the time I might want to spend more time here! But all you do is pretend you are better than I am just because you still have your job answering phones for that bigwig guy downtown!"

Katherine's parents continued to shout insults at each other as CK and Katherine listened from upstairs. CK could see the embarrassment on Katherine's face. There was nothing the girls could do to drown out the sound.

CK finally broke the ice. "It's interesting--they sound like those people we saw earlier on TV. Maybe they could get some money by working on one of those shows?" CK said, trying to be helpful since money seemed to be a big part of the current line of argument.

Katherine just shuddered. The thought that her parents could be good choices for a reality TV show with all the drama and negative energy was a difficult thought. Though she had to hand it to CK, she was probably right.

After a few minutes, the front door slammed again. Obviously, someone had left the house. A moment later, the girls heard Katherine's mom call up from downstairs.

"Katherine, are you home, dear? Did you get supper?" she asked.

"Yes Mom," Katherine answered. "I am tired and going to bed now."

"Ok – sleep well," replied her mother.

Katherine wished she could have a more normal family. She wanted to live in a household like the ones she had seen on TV where the family would sit around the table at night and have dinner together, talking about how their day went and what was happening in their life. Her family had never really been like that, even when she was young. It seemed her parents were rarely in the same room and when they were, it was just watching TV. Katherine had developed a very strong defense mechanism so people could not see how unhappy she was. She would lash out at others before they had a chance to get to know her. As a result, she didn't have a lot of friends. The girls she did hang out with were mean to other kids as well. They all tried to be cool and collected, but Katherine wondered if deep down, her "friends" hurt as badly as she did.

Katherine quickly pushed that thought out of her mind. All this self-awareness was more than she ever wanted to consider! But the bottle was open, and it was hard to keep a lid on these strange thoughts.

"I will deal with them tomorrow," she said to herself.

CK was getting very sleepy now. She was extremely tired. Katherine could see her houseguest would not make it much longer. She pulled out a sleeping bag and extra pillow for CK so she could bunk on her floor for the night. CK was very grateful. She offered up thanks to Mother Earth as she drifted off to sleep, leaving Katherine wide awake to deal with the questions that were opening up in her heart and mind. It would be a long night.

Chapter 8

ANOTHER DAY

The next morning, CK woke up early, extremely refreshed and ready for a new day. She had slept very well during the night, getting much-needed rest. She also had some lovely dreams as well. Celeste and Prog had spoken to her in her dreams, telling her everything was going to be ok and they were still with her even though she could not see them. This message was very re-assuring to CK. She knew they were there, but it was good to actually hear it.

Katherine, on the other hand, did not sleep well at all. She looked like death warmed over in the morning. She had dark circles under her eyes, and her skin had gone extremely pale, even more so than usual. Her hair was extremely rumpled as if she had been running her hands through it all night. It was obvious she had not slept much. But she did have an interesting energy around her. It felt slightly lighter than it had the day before. It was like she had lifted off a layer or two of negative energy that surrounded her. She still had a lot of work to do, but a little more understanding and self-awareness during the night had definitely done her some good, even if the lack of sleep had not.

"Good morning!" beamed CK as she awoke from her restful night's sleep.

"'Morning," mumbled Katherine in a less than excited tone.

"How did you sleep?" asked CK.

"Terrible," said Katherine. "All your questions kept me up thinking all night about my life and my friends and my family…" Her voice trailed off after this last one.

"I'm sorry," said CK. "I didn't mean to cause you any distress." Though secretly CK was glad she had posed the questions because it seemed Katherine's heart and aura were a little lighter today. "I was just trying to understand more about this world."

"Well, I guess somewhere inside I needed to think about these things," shared Katherine resigned to the fact that her world would never be the same again.

"Oh yes!" CK passionately agreed. "That's how it works! To understand ourselves and our spirit, we have to ask these deep questions and try to connect with the answers that come from our spirit and not from our ego or personality. We are so much more than this one life we are living and this one body. To try and connect with the person we really are, our higher self is such a wonderful and noble process. Only by living in alignment with our truth can we find happiness and contentment."

Katherine looked at CK with a raised eyebrow and a look of slight confusion and disbelief. First, she didn't know what a "higher self" or "ego" was. Second, she wasn't sure what CK meant by being more than this one life. Did she mean our childhood? Did she mean we have different lives at different times? It was quite confusing. And also, what did it mean to live in alignment with our truth? What's our truth? These were all pretty deep questions, and Katherine had decided she did not want to answer any more deep questions right now. Just grappling with this idea of why she put other people down and watched negative reality TV shows was more than enough for her to take in. Finding her "higher self" and living her truth would have to wait for another day.

CK could see that these concepts were a bit too much at this point in Katherine's journey. The look on her face told CK that perhaps she needed to back off the concept of a "higher self," even though CK desperately wanted to share it with her.

Everyone goes through their own journey of development and growth. At different points along that journey we are ready for different questions and to look within for answers. It is all part of the process of our soul's evolution. Most of the souls who lived in Joy-Ville were very evolved. They had already gone through these phases of self-awareness and exploration, usually in previous lives. They had come to a place where they understood that the Divine Creator connects everyone and everything in the Universe. We are all one. Most of the residents of Joy-Ville also understood the concepts of sharing and collaboration as a way to live, instead of competition. There is enough to go around for everyone, and abundance mentality is a very important aspect of living in the Fifth Dimension. And living your truth is just part of normal life there.

It was obvious to CK that many of the beings living here, in the Third Dimension, were not quite as far along in their soul's journey compared to her friends back home. This was neither good nor bad;

it just was. Everyone must follow their own path and take their own time for learning. That is part of the beautiful process of living. Everything is in perfect timing for when it is meant to be. That is probably one of the reasons CK was allowed to see the portal. It was time for some mutual growth between her and Katherine. However, these concepts were a bit much for 7am on a Saturday, and it was obvious Katherine did not want to hear about them at this point. So CK dropped the subject.

"What are you going to do today?" Katherine asked CK. "Are you going back home?"

"I need to," said CK, "but there is something I have to do first. We need to stop that metal beast from pushing down all those trees and scaring the animals. I can't leave until it is stopped."

"You can't stop a bulldozer," said Katherine. "It's not possible. They are big, and someone bought that land to build a shopping mall."

"But we have to try," implored CK. "We can't just give up."

Katherine thought for a minute. Obviously, her new foreign friend was determined to make an attempt at stopping this project. If Katherine didn't help her, she might get herself hurt.

As it happened, Katherine knew a lot about this project already. The head of the company building the mall was the mother of one of her friends from school. They had grown up together, and she spent a lot of time over at their house, especially when hers was empty. Her friend Susie might be able to help, or at least help them make an effort that would appease CK and get her to go back home.

"Ok, I have an idea," said Katherine. "Let's get dressed and go find my friend Susie. Her mom is the owner of the project to build the mall. Maybe she can help us."

CK didn't have any extra clothes with her, so Katherine loaned her one of her outfits. CK took a shower and then put on fresh clothing. She felt much better now. It was odd how the haze from the sky in this world just seemed to settle on your skin and clothes. She had never appreciated a shower so much in her life as she did today! Katherine also took a shower and got cleaned up as well.

While Katherine was showering, CK decided to meditate. She sat down quietly and created a clear intention for the outcome she wanted to happen that the bulldozer would cease to knock down any more of the trees. She knew she could make this happen. She had been taught early in her life that when we are crystal clear in our beliefs, we can make anything happen because our thoughts create action, which create our reality. CK also gave thanks to the Universe as if this event had already happened, another way to ensure that the desired outcome occurs.

After Katherine had gotten dressed, the girls went downstairs. Everything was quiet. Katherine wasn't sure if her dad had ever come home last night, but she didn't want to stick around to find out. Katherine got out another very colorful box for breakfast. This time it was from the pantry. She poured the colored cereal into two bowls and poured white liquid from the fridge on top. CK looked at the bowl with a questioning eye.

"It's cereal," said Katherine. "Haven't you ever had cereal??"

"No," said CK, "I haven't. But I am willing to try everything once and some things twice!" she smiled.

CK took a spoon and ate the cereal and milk. It was extremely sweet and had an odd taste. But CK was perfectly happy to eat it, as she was hungry again this morning.

The girls quickly finished their breakfast and went off to the playground to find Katherine's friend Susie.

Chapter 9

THE PLAYGROUND

On Saturdays, Katherine and her friends would usually meet and hang out on the playground near the school. They would use that time to get out of their houses and away from their families, and find out if there was anything interesting happening for the weekend. Today was no exception.

As Katherine and CK rounded the curve in the road, they could see a group of kids hanging out on a cement slab in the middle of the block. There were swings and slides around the area. It also had a large bridge made of old rubber tires that kids could walk across or hang on. The swings were black rubber and the slides made from shiny metal aluminum that had rusted out underneath. All in all, not a very inspirational place for creative play, at least by CK's standards. There was no grass or trees. Not even a flower pot. But there were kids playing on the old, worn-out equipment regardless, and some of them seemed to be enjoying themselves.

Susie and a few other girls were standing around talking on one side of the playground. It was obvious they were not interested in what was happening around them on the swings. They were deep in conversation about the reality TV show that was on last night, some new music that had come out and what they thought about a cute boy who had just started school last week.

Katherine and CK walked up to the group. CK could tell that Katherine was a little nervous about bringing CK with her. She was still worried about what her friends would think, even though she had a few personal revelations the night before about what did and did *not* matter. This was a breakthrough and a really big deal for Katherine to bring someone along to the group whom she had bullied just the day before. CK was very proud of Katherine's courage, though she couldn't tell her that without sounding a bit condescending. So she said nothing and just watched the scene unfold.

"Who's that!?!" asked Susie, pointing to CK. "Isn't that the weird girl who thought she was you when she came to the schoolyard yesterday? What's she doing here?"

Katherine took a deep breath. She mustered all the courage she could find at the moment to stand up to her friend. (Thankfully Prog was with her to help.)

"This is CK – she's a friend," said Katherine, trembling a bit on the inside with fear of rejection. "She is from a foreign country and didn't understand how we act here. She had never even tried pizza before, the poor thing! So I am helping her with a project before she goes back home. She's actually pretty cool."

While Katherine was introducing her to the other girls, CK intentionally sent out a beam of bright white light around each of them. She opened her heart Chakra fully, engaging each of the girls at a deeper soul level. She asked the angels and guardians to help her reach these girls and get their help to stop the metal beast. And most of all, she smiled a big grin of acceptance and love while she was meeting them.

The girls each looked at CK, glancing up and down. She didn't look too odd...at least for a foreigner. At least she was wearing normal clothes this time, thanks to borrowing some from Katherine's wardrobe.

"Where are you from?" asked Susie.

"A village called Joy-Ville" replied CK. "It's very far away, and I need to return there soon."

"Oh," replied Susie. "And why did you come here?" she asked.

"I just wanted to visit and see what this place was like. But when I came into town, I saw this metal beast, a 'bulldozer,' tearing down the trees and frightening the animals. So now I need to find a way to stop it before I return home," replied CK.

Susie looked at Katherine with a questioning look.

"She wants to stop the mall by Whale Mountain," explained Katherine. "She thinks she can convince your mom to stop tearing down the trees if she has a chance to speak with her."

Susie and the other girls looked at CK and started to laugh. They couldn't believe this girl thought she could stop something like a shopping mall from being built! How crazy was that! She must be from another planet, not just another country.

"You're crazy," said Susie. "You can't just make that happen and stop a building from going up."

Before CK could even respond, a loud scream came from the other side of the playground. A little girl had fallen off a swing and landed elbow-first on the hard black tarmac beneath the swing.

"Oh my gosh," shouted Susie, "it's Maribel! My little sister!"

All the older girls immediately stopped their conversation and went running over to see what had happened. Maribel lay on the ground sobbing, holding her elbow and arm up close to her chest. It was obvious that the arm was broken, as Maribel was holding it at a very funny angle in which it normally would not turn. The little girl was both frightened and in deep pain after falling so fast and hitting such a hard substance below her.

"Oh, Maribel! What have you done??" Susie exclaimed.

The girl just sobbed, unable to catch her breath. But it was very obvious what had happened. She had been pumping the swing going back and forth, and the rusted chains had given way to release the rubber seat while she was in mid-swing. At that point, nothing could hold on to the little girl as she landed on the cement.

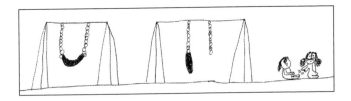

CK could feel the little girl's pain deep within her. It was excruciating. Without thinking twice about the implications of her actions, CK rushed to the girl's side. She closed her eyes, put her hands together and asked for support from the Angels to bring Reiki healing for this girl. CK could feel a rush of energy enter her body from the top of her head down to her feet. She had been "attuned" to using Reiki energy many years before and was an expert in its use. Reiki is healing energy that comes from the universe. It feels like a bright light or burst of energy. Only those who have been trained can use it. CK was one of these. In Joy-Ville Reiki was used before traditional medicine most of the time. It was very powerful at healing, and CK had a strong grasp of it.

CK rubbed her hands together and placed her palms on the top of the sobbing girl's head. She would work on the arm in a moment, but she needed Maribel to calm down and breathe, and she wanted to take some of the pain away. CK allowed the healing Reiki energy to flow into Maribel's body, trying to absorb and disperse some of the shock of the impact. She spoke quietly to Maribel, telling her to breathe slowly, close her eyes and picture her pain going away. The little girl complied. She could feel the calmness of CK's hands and energy on her head. Maribel began to calm down, catching her breath. Her arm still hurt a lot, but she was starting to feel a bit better.

Next, CK moved her hands down Maribel's neck and shoulders while she continued to send healing Reiki energy into the child's body. Maribel began to relax. She had stopped sobbing and was now able to breathe more normally, though her face was ashen from the experience.

Once CK had Maribel's pain and breathing under control, she sat down on the ground in front of the girl. It was time to work on this arm, but first she needed to get the girl to trust her.

"Maribel, that's your name, right?" CK asked quietly. The girl just nodded. She still couldn't talk.

"Maribel, I need you to help me. I am going to fix your arm, but you must trust me and help me. Can you do that?" CK asked. Maribel nodded again.

"Ok, here is what we are going to do. I am using some healing energy called Reiki, and together we are going to heal your arm. It works best if you believe in it too. Can you believe that we can make your arm all better?" CK asked.

Maribel thought about it for a moment. She was much younger than her older sister and not yet jaded by the world. She believed in magic and fairytales, and that love makes the world go around.

"Is it magic?" she asked softly, whimpering in pain.

"Yes," smiled CK, "it is magic, and it will make you all better soon."

"Ok," said Maribel, "then I can believe it too."

"Good," smiled CK. "I am going to put some of this magic into your arm, and I need you to picture it getting better."

Maribel still had her arm held up against her chest. CK placed her hands lightly on the arm. Maribel winced in pain. Bright Reiki energy shot out of CK's fingertips and palms. All the girls were standing around and could not believe their eyes. They saw bright light protruding from CK's hands and flowing into Maribel's arms. They were speechless. No one on the playground said a word. They just watched with mouths hanging open as white light flowed from CK into Maribel.

In the third dimension, there were Reiki healers who used this energy. But no one had ever seen energy that was this strong. That's probably because, in CK's home, this energy was used all the time for instant healing. In the third dimension, there was still a limiting belief that healing took time and could not be done immediately. But with Maribel's faith and CK's healing powers, the little girl was soon feeling much better.

After a few minutes of this intense Reiki treatment, Maribel was able to bend her arm again. It still hurt, and it was very sore, but it was clear the bone had been repaired, as it was no longer hanging at a strange angle and dangling loose.

"Wow!" said Susie, who had finally found her voice. "I can't believe you did that!"

CK just smiled. She knew the power of healing energy, and she was thankful for this opportunity to channel it and help this little girl.

"How did you fall?" asked a boy who had been watching the entire scene unfold.

"The swing broke, and the ground was too hard," replied Maribel.

An energetic light bulb went off in CK's head. "I've got it!" said CK. "I have an idea! Where I am from, we also have swings and playgrounds, but they are all in the trees, not outside the trees. We have hemp rope that we use to create bridges across the trees, and we make swings that hang from the branches. We don't cut down our trees; we create play inside them and work with them! Maybe your mom would consider not cutting down the rest of the trees and using them for play?" CK asked, looking at Susie and Katherine hopefully. "Look at this playground with all the metal and the hard floor. It's not safe for kids. The forest floor is much softer and more natural. Wouldn't that be much better than playing here and getting hurt?" she asked.

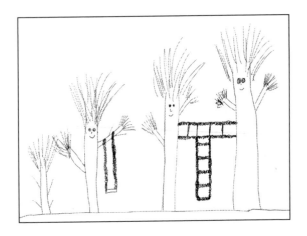

The kids on the playground looked around at each other. This was a pretty cool idea. They didn't have many trees in this part of the city, and the idea of being able to swing and play around trees sounded pretty neat.

After watching this strange lady with whiskers heal her little sister, Susie finally got over the shock, found her voice again and spoke up. "That's a really good idea. We don't want other kids hurt like Maribel was today. Let's find my mom and talk to her about this idea. They have already taken down a lot of the trees for the project, but maybe they could leave some up and make a place to play as well," Susie said.

With a renewed energy and a sense of purpose, CK, Katherine, Susie, Maribel and a few other kids from the playground went off to Susie's house to find Susie's mom.

Chapter 10

THE MALL

"MOOOMMMM…" shouted Susie and Maribel as they entered their house. "Mom, where are you??" they continued.

Their mother had been reading the paper and drinking a cup of coffee. It was early on a Saturday morning after all.

"What? What is it?" asked their mother. She could sense the level of distress in the voices of her daughters. It was the kind of subtle tone only a parent would be able to notice, but it was there.

Maribel was still holding her arm. Although it was much better than before, it still hurt. After all, going from a full break to more of a heavy bruise was pretty amazing, but there was still some healing to be done.

"I broke my arm," said Maribel, "and this girl fixed it with magic," she continued, pointing to CK. CK just smiled. "It hurt so bad, and the bone was sticking out, but now it just hurts a little bit because of the magic energy she used."

Their mom just smiled an accepting smile. She knew her daughter liked to believe in things like ghosts, fairies, and magic. But she could also see the arm was still heavily bruised, and there was some swelling around it. "So what actually happened?" she asked, turning to Susie.

"Maribel was on one of those old rusted swings. The chain broke, and she fell hard and hit her elbow on the tarmac. Maribel is right – CK did some cool energy work on her arm and made it a lot better. It looked broken before," Susie told her mother.

Susie's mom now looked at CK. *What an interesting looking child! And those hairs on her face – they almost look like whiskers! Poor kid – does she not have a home life or a mother who cares?* She thought.

Susie saw her mom looking oddly at CK and spoke up. "She's from another country, just visiting here to see our city," Susie explained, reading the questioning look on her mother's face.

Ah, thought Susie's mom, *that makes more sense then.* While their mom did not believe that CK had healed her daughter's arm with magic energy, she was still very concerned about the amount of bruising that she was seeing on the child.

Susie continued, "She had a great idea about your project out by Whale Mountain. Where she lives, they build their playgrounds inside the trees instead of cutting the trees down. We need a new playground, so no one else will get hurt like Maribel. What if we put a new playground by the mall so kids can play while their parents are shopping?" suggested Susie.

Her mother paused for a moment to consider the suggestion.

CK finally spoke up. "In my home, we use things like hemp rope for the swings that protect the trees so they can still grow and live but we can also play on them. The ground is soft soil where you land and walk, and the trees provide shade on sunny days. We don't use things like metal that can rust and turn orange. We use more natural substances that work with the trees instead of destroying them." CK took a breath. She could see Susie's mom was still thinking about this idea.

Katherine decided to add a few thoughts of her own. "Ya know, it would be great for business because parents could bring their kids to play and maybe there could even be a place they can sit and talk under the trees. I'm sure they will be thirsty or hungry, so they can go to the mall to get drinks and food while the kids are playing. More business for you, safe play for the kids. We call that a 'win/win' in debate class," Katherine added.

Their mom continued to ponder the request of the children.

Finally, Maribel also piped in. "Please Mom, I don't want to get hurt anymore. CK might not be here next time to fix me, and I will have to go to the doctor."

This comment was the final blow. All the walls and barriers came down. Tears flooded their mom's eyes as she thought about her girls getting hurt on the old playground and having to go to the hospital or worse.

"Ok," she said. "Let's go out to the site and look at where a playground might fit in."

The girls all cheered and piled into their mom's car to drive out to the site where the metal beast had been tearing down trees. CK was so excited by the idea of stopping the beast; she didn't even notice how odd it felt to ride inside this tin box for transportation. Oh, how she wished she could just think about where she wanted to go and just show up there. But that didn't seem to be as easy in this land as it was in the Fifth Dimension. So for now, a car would have to do.

The group arrived at the building site. The metal beast of a bulldozer was asleep. It was Saturday, and the driver had the day off. CK was glad to see nothing was being torn down right now--what a relief!

As they got out of the car, CK could see how much destruction the bulldozer had already done, and it made her heart very sad. Where the bulldozer had been, there was nothing left but red clay. Not a tree anywhere in the area. However, CK also saw there were still a lot of trees still standing right in the bulldozer's path. Perhaps that would be the best option for a tree playground.

CK went up to Susie's mom. "You need a lot of space for a tree playground," she recommended. "I think this whole area would be perfect. Kids could play hide and seek. You could put up some swings from these branches," she said, pointing to some large oaks in the mix. "And the more trees you leave in place, the more shade offered."

The Mall

Susie's mom pulled out a large map from her car. It was the blueprint of the shopping mall she planned to build. She could see the stores committed, where she planned for various shops and the future extensions. She nodded her head in agreement.

"Actually, that's a great idea. If I cut off this part of the mall and make a few stores a little smaller, I can use this land for a playground instead," she said, pointing to an area on the blueprint. It was the same area where the bulldozer now sat, waiting to start back up on Monday morning.

"I will call Jack this weekend and let him know we have a change of plans. We are not going to knock them over, but instead, design a playground around them. Thank you, girls, for this great idea! I know it will be a huge hit and I have you all to thank for it!" exclaimed Susie's mom.

"Oh no," said Susie, "it was all CK's idea. She's the one that wanted to save the trees and find a safer place to play."

"It was all her idea," the girls agreed.

"Well CK, then I have you to thank," said their mom. "I know you are from a foreign country, but I would like you to come back and visit when we are finished." With that, Susie's mom took out her pocketbook and handed CK several pieces of green paper.

"This is just some money, so when you come back to visit, you can buy some food and have some fun and enjoy the playground, my treat!"

"Thank you," said CK, not sure what this green paper was. "I truly appreciate it," she said. Even though she didn't know how money was used, a gift given with love was always appreciated, regardless of what it actually contained.

Katherine could see CK looked a bit confused. "It's money," she told her quietly. "You use it to buy things you need at the mall or anywhere else in the city."

"Ok, thanks," said CK, pretending to understand completely. She did get the concept of barter. You give them green paper for what you need. She just wasn't sure how much green paper she would need to use. It didn't really matter, though. She was now planning to go back home to Joy-Ville, so it would be fun to show this green "money" to Mr. Tortoise and her friends! What a fabulous souvenir!

"Time to go," said Susie's mom. "Everybody back in the car."

"Actually, I am visiting very close to here," said CK. "So I think I will stay and then head back home."

"You're not coming?" asked Katherine.

"No," said CK. "My work here is done," she smiled.

Katherine gave CK a huge hug. She gave her some information called an email address on a piece of paper and asked CK to send her a letter. CK was not sure she could send a letter, but took the paper anyway and mumbled an acceptance.

Maribel and Susie also gave CK a big hug and thanked her for healing Maribel. CK was glad to do it.

As the car drove away, CK found herself once again surrounded by mounds of giant red clay. She then turned and look out at the trees that would now be safe from destruction. Interestingly enough, she could no longer hear their cries or feel the fear of the animals in the trees. *How odd,* CK thought. *Now they just look like trees. I don't feel any emotion from them.* Although she didn't realize it at the time, this was not a good thing for CK. Her lack of ability to hear the trees or feel the animals meant that her vibration had dropped even lower than it had been the day before. Not only could she not see or hear Prog, Celeste, and Nana Whiskers, now she could not hear or speak to the trees.

"It's time to go home," she said aloud to no one in particular. And with that, CK started walking toward Whale Mountain to find her spinning portal and go home.

Chapter 11

WHALE MOUNTAIN

As Cosmic Kitty approached Whale Mountain, things seemed a bit different. She could not believe that it was only 24 hours previously when she had arrived in this crazy place. She missed her friends and family back in Joy-Ville, and she wondered if they missed her as well. Unfortunately, the hazy color of the sky seemed more normal now, and she had stopped trying to talk with her friend Sunny the day before since he wouldn't answer. It was definitely time to go home!

She looked around the mountain to find the door to the portal where she had entered the third dimension. All she saw on the side of the mountain was rock and stone. She walked toward some bushes that seemed familiar. Then she walked over behind another crevice she recognized. CK continued to search for almost 30 minutes, but she could not find the blurring, round spinning door anywhere!

"I know it's here!" she said out loud. "It has to be!"

The more she continued to look, the more concerned she became. This portal was her only way home! Oh, how she wished she could speak to Celeste, Prog and Nana Whiskers! They would help her figure out why the door would not open for her.

CK sat down on a rock to think. Oddly enough, it was the same rock she sat on when she first came through the portal the day before and officially met her spirit guides! How ironic. But this time, there was no spinning portal to be found. And thankfully, no loud bulldozer either, thanks to CK's efforts!

But still, how would she get home?

If only I could speak to Celeste and Prog, they would tell me what to do and show me the way, she thought. She sat quietly for a while longer, trying to get any communication she could receive from them.

Suddenly an idea popped into her head. When CK entered the city yesterday, she had seen a sign for a psychic medium in one of the shops she had passed. *That's it!* She thought. *I will work with someone who can connect with Nana Whiskers and my guides and have a conversation on what I should do!*

A psychic medium is someone who can speak to people or beings on other planes of existence. All people have the ability to connect to other dimensions, and do it regularly with guides, departed loved ones and even with higher selves. But a psychic medium is someone who practices and can do it "on command." That said, the clarity of the communication at any given point can be very good or very bad. For a psychic to connect with beings in higher realms, they must raise their vibration up to "hear" better. At the same time, the departed loved ones must bring their vibration down to get their message across clearly. It is never easy to communicate and often messages are misheard or only partially received. Some psychics practice and manage their energy and vibration better than others. Think of it like singing. Some people have more raw talent and some people practice like crazy to build their skill. But in the end, everyone can sing. Some just do it better than others, either because of talent or practice. It's the same with psychic ability. Some people have a more natural connection or practice to build it, but everyone can connect with other realms at some level; and often do it without even realizing it – that's called intuition.

Cosmic Kitty felt that a third dimensional psychic might be able to help her speak with Nana Whiskers and her guides so she could get some help.

As she walked back toward the city, back up the big hill using the sidewalk, she could see the lights and buildings, as she once again crested the same hill she had covered the day before. *How much difference a day makes,* she thought to herself. *The last time I did this, I was in search of myself. Now, I have not only stopped the metal beast as planned, but I also gave the "me" in this dimension more to think about on her journey.* CK was very happy and proud of her accomplishments in this world. She couldn't wait to get home and tell everyone about it!

As she walked back into the city, this time she managed to avoid the cars. She was a kitty woman on a mission as she zig-zagged through the streets to figure out where she had seen that window sign for a psychic. A large blinking light told her she was in the right place. "Madam Zorba," the sign read "Psychic medium, tarot reader, and counselor." This was it. CK took a deep breath and walked in.

Chapter 12

MADAM ZORBA

As CK walked into the dimly lit shop, she had trouble deciding if this was a good idea or not. Part of her thought it would be helpful but part of her also worried that perhaps this lady might not help her. Her intuition had kicked in, and she began to question whether this was a true psychic or a fake, but CK progressed anyway, desperate for any chance to find her way home.

"Welcome dear," said a voice from behind the counter. "How can we help you today?"

"I would like help talking to my spirit guides and Grandmother," said CK.

"Certainly," said the voice, "we can do that. Readings are $125 per hour."

"I don't think I need that much time," said CK. "I am trying to get home and hopefully I can get the information I need faster than that. Usually, I can hear it myself, but today I feel blocked for some reason," CK confessed.

"That's fine," said the voice. "You can go in and see Madam Zorba, and we'll figure out how long it takes. Are you paying with cash or card?" she asked. CK had no idea what the lady was talking about. Then she remembered the green paper Susie's mom had given her to come back and "shop" when the mall was open.

"This green stuff ok?" CK asked, holding out the money.

The voice giggled and said, "Yes, dear."

CK was pointed toward the back of the store through an open door at the end of a long hallway. The light was still low, but she could see paintings on the wall and large rolls of velvet cloth everywhere. She walked through the door and sat down at the table with Madam Zorba.

She is a reader?!? CK asked herself. She looked at this lady who had on brightly colored clothes and more paint and color on her face than CK had ever seen. CK knew a lot of people who could connect with higher realms in her world. They were very spiritual people. They looked just like everyone else, but they spent a lot of time in meditation and used their gifts to help others on their journey. This lady did not look like any reader CK had ever seen, but she was willing to try.

CK sat down on a pink overstuffed stool and pulled up to a round table.

"Welcome," said Madam Zorba, "what are you looking for today?" Madam Zorba also thought CK looked a little odd. What strange whiskers on her face. *She must be from out of town,* she concluded.

"I am trying to get home," CK told her, "but I need the help of my grandmother and my life and protector guides to tell me how to get there."

Madam Zorba nodded her head in understanding. "I see," she said, "so you are trying to get back to where?"

"My home in Joy-Ville," CK replied, not wanting to give too much information, as she didn't want to influence the information the reader might get.

"Joy-Ville!" laughed Madam Zorba. "What a funny name – that must be a lovely and fun place!" she continued sarcastically.

"It is," replied CK. "It's fabulous, and I miss it a lot. Can you help me get there?" she asked.

"Well dear," replied Madam Zorba, "we'll see what spirits are with us today and if they are willing to help you get home. Just relax, and I'll do everything."

CK took a deep breath and tried to relax. She was very tense and anxious about connecting with her guides. She knew that it was not helpful to worry, and everything would work out as it was supposed to, but it was harder than usual to keep calm.

Madam Zorba lit a white candle in the middle of the table. She said a quick protection prayer and then she invited any beings here to help CK to come forth at this time.

Above Madam Zorba's head, Celeste, Prog, and Nana Whiskers began to appear. Neither CK nor Madam Zorba could physically see them, but Madam Zorba could hear something "coming into tune" around her; she could feel a new energy.

"Is this the person who is going to help us!?!" Prog almost shouted. "Look at her! What's with all that makeup? Does she work as a clown during off hours, entertaining children?"

"Calm down," offered Celeste. "I know this is not one of the best psychics we have ever come across, but let's see if we can get some messages through her to help CK get home."

"But she is not even in channel!" protested Prog. "She didn't even connect up to her OWN guides to ask for help!"

"I know," said Celeste, "but we'll find a way for her to understand."

What Prog was talking about was the way that most psychics connect with beings in higher dimensions. The usual process was to say a prayer of protection, asking for guidance and help from Archangels, usually toward the four corners of the Earth (north, south, east, and west). The psychic would usually surround themselves with positive energy and go up through a tube of white light to connect and see/hear their guides. This was called "being in channel." From there they can also talk to other spirits who have crossed over on behalf of the person for whom they are reading. For those who can see energy easily, an actual channel or tube of light can be seen coming from the top of the crown chakra of the psychic (the top of the head) and going up into the Heavens if the psychic is truly connected and communicating with beings and spirits on other planes. In this case, Madam Zorba was not properly connected to her own spirit guides, much less other beings. However, Celeste, Prog, and Nana Whiskers were intent on trying to reach CK and communicate with Madam Zorba. Since she was not in channel, it would take a lot more energy and effort to get through to her. They would have to reach her on her level in the third dimension.

"I feel a presence here," moaned Madam Zorba as if in a trance state. "The spirits are definitely with us here today....."

CK just looked around the room. She didn't feel or hear anything unusual, and she was pretty in tune with new energy. Of course, she wouldn't feel a new energy with her spirit guides because they were always with her anyway.

"I sense a grandmother coming through..." Madam Zorba continued.

"Yes! Yes!" said CK. "That's her!"

"She's wearing a black dress and holding a pocketbook. She is showing me money in her purse, indicating that she is glad you are here to get help!" Madam Zorba moaned.

"Um...I don't think that's her," said CK. "My grandmother doesn't know anything about this green stuff called 'money.' We didn't have any of it where we lived."

"In the afterlife dear, our loved ones know about everything. All things become clear, even things they never had," Madam Zorba explained. CK was not sure she believed Madam Zorba, but she decided not to protest and just see what else she could find out.

"What else is she saying?" asked CK. "Does she know how I should get home?"

"It's hard to connect with her clearly," said Madam Zorba. "Now she is showing me some pies and cookies; she wants to share them with you."

CK did not even know what a pie or a cookie was, much less why her grandmother would want her to have them. "Um – I don't think that's her," said CK. "Maybe we should try something else?"

Madam Zorba just moaned louder as if going into a deeper trance.

Above Zorba's head, Celeste and Prog started screaming as loud as they could, "CARDS!! CARDS!! USE the CARDS!!"

Madam Zorba took a deep breath, closed her eyes and began to concentrate. She heard a tiny voice in her ear shouting, "Cards! Cards!" She opened her eyes and looked at CK. "I feel drawn to pull a few cards," she said slowly and deliberately.

By this, Madam Zorba meant that she was going to pull some Tarot cards to see what messages she could find in them for Cosmic Kitty. Cards made CK very happy. She had studied Tarot cards last year when she was taking a course in the history of metaphysical studies. A lot of her friends who did readings regularly also used the cards as a way to get more information or clarify information they were already getting from Spirit.

Tarot cards are meant to represent the stages of life. The major arcana are big milestones through the course of a specific journey. For example, everyone always starts a new journey in the beginning as "The Fool." This is not a negative term; it is actually quite positive, indicating innocence and being naïve about the journey about to be started. Along the way one encounters different stages, from manifestation with the Magician to the Lovers for new relationships to the Moon for coming into psychic powers and finally ending with the World, for completion. There are 22 different cards in this major life journey. There is also the minor Arcana, which is all about smaller nuances and shifts in life. There are 56 cards in the Minor Arcana, made up of four suits: Wands, Cups, Swords, and Pentacles. They also stand for different day-to-day activities in life. Tarot cards will show the direction someone is currently headed, but they are not meant to predict the future. Only the person who is being read can make the decisions that will create the outcome desired. The cards are only meant to show the current direction if nothing changes. Sometimes just doing a reading and getting the knowledge needed can change the direction someone is headed. That is why no two readings are ever the same, even on the same person.

CK knew all of this. She knew that the cards could serve as great messages on what you should do and the current direction. So she was excited that Madam Zorba had gotten a message to use them.

From her side table, Madam Zorba picked up a deck of cards. They were like no other deck CK had ever seen. They had cartoon characters on them! *How odd,* thought CK. *These seem to have some of the same characters I have seen in some of my story books at home.*

Above Madam Zorba's head, Prog was livid. "Really?? Is she using Tarot cards with Disney characters on them?" he asked, incensed.

"Yes," said Celeste, "she is. Now hush so we can figure out how to use these cards to get our message across."

Nana Whiskers, hanging nearby, had begun to fidget and play with her hands. She wanted this to work, as she too was ready to return to Joy-Ville. Celeste and Prog may have spent time helping Katherine in the third dimension, but Nana Whiskers did not have that many memories of being in this place, and she didn't think she wanted anymore. Besides, she couldn't believe this woman said she was dressed in a black dress! That was silly! Who wears black when they leave the body!? That's just too dark!

Madam Zorba shuffled the deck of cards. "Shuffle again" came a low voice in her ear, so she continued. "Cut the deck" came another voice, so she did as she heard. Finally, she heard Celeste whisper, "Draw."

Madam Zorba stopped shuffling and laid three cards out on the table.

The first card was Ursula, from the story "The Little Mermaid."* Ursula is the sea witch who convinced Ariel (the mermaid) to make a deal and trade her voice for legs to win the heart of a prince. The second card was Elsa, from the story "Frozen."* Elsa was the queen who had the ability to freeze things and had to use love instead of fear to figure out how to control her power and use it for good. To succeed, she had to let go of the fear and bring in the love. The final card was the Genie from the story, "Aladdin."* The Genie gave Aladdin three wishes and helped him beat the bad guys and rescue

---

* Disney released the Little Mermaid in an animated movie in 1989; Disney released Frozen in an animated movie in 2013; Disney released Alladin in an animated movie in 1992

the kingdom after Aladdin had learned his lesson about telling the truth and being honest about who you truly are.

CK wasn't sure what to make of these cards. She needed to understand what they stood for in the traditional Tarot deck.

Madam Zorba looked over the cards carefully. CK asked her to please tell her what she saw and what the card stood for in the normal tarot spread.

"Well," started Madam Zorba, "Ursula stands for the devil in the traditional deck. Have you been making deals with the devil? Is that what brought you here?" she asked indignantly.

"No! Absolutely not!" shouted CK. "I come from a very peaceful place, and we don't make deals like that!"

"Then maybe it means you came from the sea since Ursula is a sea witch?" Madam Zorba continued.

"What the heck is she talking about!?" screamed Prog. "She has no idea what these cards mean. Is she even trained in card reading at all?! What IS her deal?"

"Hang on," said Celeste. "Let's see if CK can figure this out. Just wait."

CK looked at Madam Zorba and wrinkled her nose and whiskers. "I did not come from the sea, nor do I need to go home back to the sea. However, if this is the devil card, for me it represents negativity. The devil is about fear, which is a low vibration energy. When you are caught in low vibration energy, it is very hard to see what is really there. It can be hard to see the good things because you are looking at the bad. You feel trapped by negativity, but the reality is that you have trapped yourself usually. You are allowing yourself to experience or feel the negative energy around you." CK paused to think. "That's what it means! It stands for negative energy and low vibration!" CK exclaimed, proud of herself that she realized this card was not about going home to the sea or making a deal with the devil. She would have to thank her friend Ninyette for that great piece of knowledge they had just been discussing recently.

"If you say so," said Madam Zorba, still not convinced the girl in front of her should not head for the ocean. She continued, "The second card is Elsa from 'Frozen.' She is used to represent the Eight of Cups. This card is about being cold. Is your home a cold place? Especially combined with water, it seems like these are about going back somewhere wet and cold," Madam Zorba began.

"What!?!" Prog practically screamed. "Water! Being cold! This woman has no clue what these cards mean or how we are using them."

Prog was furious. With all the energy he could muster, he started pushing energy into the light hanging over her head. It began to flicker on and off until he was tired and out of breath from creating movement in the third-dimensional world. It takes a lot of energy for a spirit to make something happen on the physical plane. First, they must lower their vibration to the world they want to touch, and then they must pull in or push energy to move objects. It's exhausting. But Prog had managed to get the light to flicker several times.

"See," said Madam Zorba, "the spirits agree with me!"

"UGH!" moaned Prog. "I give up. We need another way to reach CK – let's get her out of here."

"Patience, Prog," said Celeste, "have faith. Our CK can figure this out. She's smart and intuitive. She knows these are the wrong answers and she will figure out the right ones."

"I don't come from a cold place," stated CK. "Actually, it's quite sunny and warm. I don't think that's the meaning of this card for me. But you said it's the Eight of Cups, correct? That card is all about letting go and walking away from something. Success through release."

In the background, Nana Whiskers started singing the soundtrack for the movie "Frozen." The words "Let it go, Let it go, Can't hold it back anymore, Let it go, Let it go, turn away and slam the door" began to echo in CK's ears. She knew this song. It was on one of her movies from home.

"That's it!" CK exclaimed, almost jumping out of her chair. "I have to let go of fear and invite love in. I have to 'let it go, let it go,'" she stated, as she started to sing the song from the movie that was stuck in her head.

CK stopped in her tracks. "What fear? What should I be letting go of to get home?" she asked out loud, more to herself than to Madam Zorba. She wasn't afraid of anything, to be honest. She wanted to go home, yes, but she was not afraid.

Hmm…let it go, let it go, CK thought. *How does that work with the devil card?* Suddenly an idea popped into her mind. CK figured it out. The devil card, played by Ursula, was negativity and low vibration. The Elsa card for the Eight of Cups was the "let it go" card. So what the two together meant was that she needed to let go of the negativity and low vibration! That's it! She needed to raise her vibration to release herself from this dimension! She had it! Now it all made sense. If she could not see Celeste, Prog, and Nana Whiskers because her vibration had dropped, then that is probably why she could not see and use the portal as well! After all, Joy-Ville probably didn't want people from the Third Dimension wandering into the fifth dimension. So only those beings who were already vibrating at the high frequency of love found in the fifth dimension could see and use the portal! Wow! That's it! But how…how should she get her vibration up?

Madam Zorba looked at Cosmic Kitty with a funny look on her face. What was this girl rambling on about? Portals? Joy-Ville? Fifth dimension? It was time to finish this reading and move on. Another client was waiting.

"That's nice, dear," said Madam Zorba in a condescending tone. "Let's finish up here, though, shall we?"

"Yes," CK agreed. She too was done with this woman who wanted to send her off to a cold ocean somewhere.

The third card in the spread was the Genie from the movie Aladdin. "This card is the Genie, and it represents the Nine of Cups. The Genie means you are going to get a wish," shared Madam Zorba. Finally, something CK could agree with. The Nine of Cups was considered the "wish fulfillment" card in CK's world. It means the outcome of the question is positive. If CK was able to let go of the negativity based on the first two cards, this third card said that she would have her wish fulfilled, which was to go home. CK was ecstatic! This was great news!

She thanked Madam Zorba and rushed out of the room. She had to figure out how to raise her vibration back to the level of the fifth dimension so she could find the portal doorway. Of course, the voice at the front door stopped her and collected some of that green paper from her pocket to pay for services, but CK didn't care because she knew what she needed to do.

Meanwhile, Celeste, Prog, and Nana Whiskers still floated above Zorba as her next client came in.

"Hello dear," Madam Zorba started as her next customer sat down.

Prog stuck his tongue out at Madam Zorba as the three left to join CK.

"That wasn't very nice," said Celeste.

"She's a fraud," retorted Prog. "Her karma will find her later."

"Perhaps," said Celeste, "but it's not our place to judge her journey. This may be something she needs to experience as part of her life lesson. Hopefully, she will one day learn to use her God-given intuition more properly."

"We can always hope," chimed in Nana Whiskers, as they caught up to CK in the street.

Chapter 13

GOOD VIBRATIONS

Celeste and Prog were relieved that CK had figured out their message, even with a less than skillful messenger in the mix. Now they had to figure out other ways to help CK to raise her vibration. If she could get her soul and body back to the frequency of the fifth dimension, she would be able to see her guides and also the spinning portal.

Prog was beginning to get concerned. It was getting later in the day, and he was worried CK would not have a place to sleep if she had to stay in this city another night. Celeste was not as concerned. She knew that Cosmic Kitty was tenacious. When she decided to do something, she would go at it 100%. Celeste was certain that CK would be able to raise her vibration before it got too dark to find the portal door.

As CK walked down the street after leaving Madam Zorba, she started to think.

How do I get my vibration up? What does that even mean? In my world, high vibration is just normal. It's how we live. I don't have to work at it at all. It just happens. With all of these thoughts, CK started to frown.

She realized she wasn't sure HOW to raise her vibration significantly, especially in this world. At home when she wanted to be happier, she would visit her friends, and they would laugh and have fun and play. That gave her positive energy. She would also meditate near a high energy vortex when she wanted to reach up into higher planes of existence. That would raise her vibration as well. But neither of those things were available to her here in the third dimension.

"Think, think...or you will be trapped," she said to herself.

CK continued to walk down the street. She got a strange feeling in her gut that she should turn left. She didn't know why, but since she didn't know where she was headed anyway, left seemed as good a direction as any.

As she walked down the street, CK could feel a strong negative energy of worry come over her. She decided she needed to stop and calm herself down. She needed to relax. She would not be able to raise her vibration if she could not get this negative thinking out of her mind. After another block of walking, CK found a bench on the sidewalk. It was old and weathered. Obviously, it had been there a while. She sat down to collect her thoughts and meditate. She needed to dismiss some of this negative thinking before she could even begin to focus on raising her vibration. She sat on the bench, closed her eyes and brought bright, beautiful white light down from the heavens into her body. She allowed thoughts to enter her mind and then easily dismissed them and pushed them out. Only positive and uplifting feelings were allowed to stay. She also began to breathe slowly, counting the breaths along the way to give her mind something to focus on. Each time she got to 10 breaths, she would start counting over again back at one to make sure she was focused on breathing and not on other things. She pictured the white light coming down through her body and radiating out to others around her. She felt calm and even a bit happy as she finally opened her eyes slowly, back to the bench on which she sat.

As CK opened her eyes, she heard a cough behind her. She quickly looked around to see an older gentleman sitting in the doorway on the ground behind the bench. His clothes were ragged and he looked like life had been a bit tougher on him than most. CK was surprised to see him there. Had he been there the whole time and she did not even notice? It wasn't like her not to see another being in her presence.

"Hello, I'm CK," she said with a smile. The warm glow of meditation still made CK feel giddy and she shined both inside and out.

"Hi," said the man in the doorway. He didn't offer his name. But he couldn't believe this strange-looking young lady was not only speaking to him but looking at him directly and even making eye contact. Most people looked away when they saw him. They didn't see his sweet spirit or the glow behind his heart. They just saw the ragged clothes and refused to acknowledge him. This odd girl with whiskers actually introduced herself!

"I'm Ralph," he finally offered, returning her introduction with a faint smile. "Were you sleeping?" he sheepishly asked her, referencing her time in meditation.

"Oh no," CK smiled. "I was meditating. It's a way for me to connect with a higher vibration and also clear my head of negative thinking," she continued.

"Oh," said Ralph. "That sounds interesting. I could use some of that clarity."

With that, CK began to explain to him just how to meditate. She explained the breathing techniques, counting to 10, allowing thoughts to enter but easily pushing them out, picturing white light and most of all, not getting frustrated or judging if you don't seem to get it right away.

"It takes time and practice," she explained. "It took me years before I could easily get into a meditation and stay there without a bunch of extra thoughts coming in. I still have to work at it some days. But that's part of the benefit – the practice."

Ralph took it all in. He was much more spiritual than he realized and this little girl had reminded him of some important things he knew but had forgotten. Life living on the street had not been easy and connecting with Spirit could be a challenge when your most pressing issue is where your next meal would come from. But the reality is that this is when you most need your connection to Spirit and a belief that God is here and you are not alone. This chat was a wonderful reminder for Ralph that he was truly a child of the Universe and part of the Divine. Meeting CK had opened up his heart and reminded him that he, like all of us, is truly worthy.

CK looked up at the sky. The sun was moving, and she needed to get going. She felt lighter and more energetic. But she still didn't see her guides or Nana Whiskers, so she had to keep going.

She gave Ralph a hug, wished him well and off she went to seek more high vibrations.

Chapter 14

THE STORE

As CK walked along the block, she again felt like she needed to turn left.

"Haven't I done this already?" she asked herself.

The answer popped into her head. "Yes. But do it again."

"Ok," said CK, and she turned left. She was used to following directions that often seemed to come out of nowhere.

Just at that moment, CK passed an interesting-looking shop. It had stones and bottles of oil sitting in the window. There were also several books and even some charms hanging up near the curtains.

A loud voice in her head said, "Stop! Go in!" So CK listened, not sure why she wanted to step foot into this shop, but definitely drawn to it.

As she entered through the wooden door, the strong smell of incense and sage filled her nose and mouth.

Wow, she thought. *Someone has been going a little crazy with the candles in here! Oh – candles and oils! That's it!*

CK remembered that she once read that oils and burning sage were used to clear negative energy from people. It was not used much in her world, as there was very little negative energy to begin with, but she recalled reading about it at one point. And this little shop was steaming with it!

There were samples everywhere. Bottles of oils were marked "tester," and there were oil diffusers releasing the high vibration scents into the air through mixing water and oils together to make steam.

Essential oils come from different flowers and plants. The essence is distilled from the plant leaf or stem (usually with steam or water), and then it can be used for many things, from changing energy to medical uses. For example, lavender is known for calming the user, while peppermint can give you a quick, positive energy boost. Many different oils are used for everything from a cough to skin conditions as well.

CK continued to wander around the shop. She walked past the essential oil diffusers, taking a deep breath in as she passed. She walked through a doorway into another part of the shop. There she found samples of sage where customers could practice burning sage and smell the different flavors offered. CK picked up a white sage sample and turned it over in her hand. The dried sage leaves had been tied together with string to make it easier to burn.

"Use the shell and the feather," came a sweet voice from the shadows.

The Store

CK turned around to see an older, kind-looking woman standing beside her. She was slightly taller than CK, with long silver hair. Feathers hung loosely from barrettes holding her hair back. Her outfit looked very different from the clothes CK was wearing and even different from the clothing they wore in Joy-Ville. Her clothes were woven in various colors with fringe at the bottom. She also had leather moccasins on, though CK did not know that was the name.

The woman spoke again. "If you light the sage, you can use the abalone shell to catch the ashes and the feather to move the smoke in the direction where you want it to go. 'Smudging' calls on the spirit of sacred plants to clear away the negative energy and put you and your environment back into balance and harmony," the woman explained. "You seem to need more balance and harmony perhaps?" she offered.

CK decided this was a good idea. She lit the sage, and it began to smoke heavily. CK passed the smoking bundle of tied sage around her body, over her head and neck.

Above CK and out of sight, Prog began to cough. "That's a lot of sage!" he exclaimed. They had been guiding CK to come into this particular shop. He and Celeste knew that if they could help CK to find her way in here, they could get her some additional help on how to raise her vibration. They were right.

The woman just smiled at CK as CK also coughed at the strength of the sage. But when she was done, CK felt much better. She felt like more of the weight had been lifted, and she could breathe a bit lighter again.

"Thank you for showing me how to use this," she said to the older woman.

"You are very welcome," the lady replied in a calm, soothing voice and gave CK a nod.

CK decided to see what other wisdom this woman might possess.

"Umm...can I ask you a question, please?" she started.

"Certainly," replied the woman, her feathers casually drifting around her hair.

"I am trying to raise my vibration to a much higher level. Do you have any thoughts on how I could do that quickly?" CK asked.

The wise lady just smiled. "It comes from within," she replied in her calm and assuring voice.

"I know," said CK, "but is there a way to speed it up?" she asked.

The lady just laughed again. "You must start inside, but there are a few things that might also help. You have already started by clearing away negative energy with the sage--a good start. There are also high vibration oils and crystals you can use when you meditate to help raise your vibration. Rose oil is the highest frequency oil you can buy. It resonates at 320 megahertz."

CK didn't know if 320megahertz was high enough for the fifth dimension, but it certainly could not hurt!

The wise lady continued, "You can also call on the power of certain stones. Everything in this world has a frequency or vibration to it. Some are higher than others, including the stones. Quartz crystal is a very high clearing stone that vibrates at a high frequency. Herkimer diamonds are a type of stone that is also high in frequency. So is Moldavite, which came to earth from space. Keeping these in your pocket or close to you will help your vibration."

After pausing for a moment, the lady went on, "You can also raise your vibration through sound. Come this way."

She led CK to another part of the shop where many different bowls sat around on a table. The bowls were beautiful! Some were white or colored crystal. Others were gold. They were all different sizes and sat on various stands.

The woman picked up what looked like a stick and began rubbing it around the top of one of the crystal bowls. An amazing sound came out! It was a ringing sound, but it hit CK down in the deepest part of her heart and chest. She could FEEL the vibration that was coming out of this bowl! It was amazing! As the lady continued to run the mallet around the edge of the crystal bowl, CK could feel her emotions and energetic state rising to meet the frequency of the sound. What a wonderful feeling!

CK said a quick prayer of gratitude and thanks to the universe. She felt very happy and joyful listening to this new musical instrument. As the woman continued to play, CK slowly breathed deeply, taking in all the vibration and beautiful sound being offered. She was in bliss.

When the woman finished playing, CK thanked her profusely. She felt much better now after listening to the music. Now that she had cleared her energy and listened to bowls, it was time to get some of those stones and oils the lady had told her about.

CK wandered into another part of the shop where rows and rows of plastic bins held stones and crystals of every shape and color. CK had never seen so many rocks in one place! And certainly not sorted by type! Wow!

Thankfully the bins were carefully labeled, and they were even in alphabetical order. CK was able to find a quartz crystal, Herkimer diamond and a small piece of Moldavite in a little baggie. She held the three stones in her hand, and she could feel the pulsing energy coming from them. This was a very good sign! They would certainly help bring up her vibration.

CK then made her way back to the front of the shop, where the essential oils were still burning and diffusing into the air. The thick scent of oils surrounded CK once again as she got to the front. Rose oil was the highest frequency oil she could buy. She found a very, very tiny bottle of it. She didn't need a lot, as it was very strong. It was also quite expensive, though she didn't know the true value of the green paper she would have to hand over to buy it.

So CK had her stones, she had her oil and she had listened to some high vibration sounds and been 'smudged.' Whew – that was a lot. As she went up to the front register to pay for her selections, CK noticed a rack with a bunch of magazines, books, and records. One of the magazines had pictures of red rocks on the cover and a title over them that said: "15 ways to raise your vibration."

Fantastic! Thought CK. *Thank you so much to my guides, God, the Angels and Ascended Masters! Thank you for the marvelous gift!*

CK took the magazine off the shelf and added it to her pile. Once the total was calculated, CK handed over more of the green paper and took in return a little bag with her prizes inside. She clutched her bag fiercely, guarding it with her life. She would need all of this to get back home!

Finally, CK left the unusual shop. It was truly an experience and one she would have to tell her friends about! She wondered about the interesting elderly lady who had been so helpful. Did she work at the shop or was she just another customer who was willing to share? It didn't matter because either way, CK was very grateful for her help!

With bag in hand, CK decided it was time to start heading back to the portal. Sunny was moving farther down in the sky, and she wanted to be able to see the portal once she got her vibration back up. CK walked back out of the city and up the hill. She continued, walking toward Whale Mountain and, she hoped, toward home.

Chapter 15

WHALE MOUNTAIN...AGAIN

As CK got closer to the top of the hill where the mall would be, she turned left to wander through the trees on her way back. The trees always gave CK a lot of energy. She felt their deep connection to Mother Earth and the grounding presence they possessed. After her meditation and talk with Ralph and her time in the shop, CK was feeling a bit brighter. Her mood had shifted to one of hope, and her step had more bounce in it. She could feel energy moving around inside her, still resonating from the vibration of the crystal bowls.

CK stopped for a moment in the forest. She took the time to look at each tree individually and to be thankful for it. She noticed the birds, squirrels and even a little chipmunk sitting on the ground staring back at her. She said "hello" to the chipmunk, and interestingly enough, he nodded back and scampered away.

Wow, CK thought, *did he hear me or was that my imagination?* As CK became much more present in the moment, she could just make out a little bit of the energy of the trees and some restless sounds coming through the wind. A faint "thank you" seemed to pass over her ears and heart. She wasn't completely sure it was the trees speaking to her, but she definitely felt love surrounding her in the wind. Perhaps it was also Nana Whiskers and her Guides she was feeling too. A warmth passed over her as she walked through the trees that just earlier that day, she had helped to save.

CK approached Whale Mountain. She still could not see the spinning portal, though she looked again. She felt she was definitely at a much higher vibration than she had been previously that day, but it still did not seem to be high enough.

CK sat back down on the rock where she had first met her Guides, confident this was the exact location where she needed to be to see the portal.

She opened up her bag. She was getting thirsty and hungry, but that would have to wait. She needed to get home first.

From her bag, CK pulled out the stones. Her clear quartz and Herkimer diamond sparkled in the rays of sunlight coming over the mountain. It was amazing how bright they were! The small piece of dark greenish-gray Moldavite was not nearly as pretty, but its translucent edges caught the sunshine as well. CK put all three stones in her hand, closed her eyes and said a prayer of intention, asking that these stones help her to raise her vibration so she could return home. Once her prayer was done, she put the stones in her pocket so they could stay close to her body.

Next, CK pulled out the Rose essential oil. The lady had told her the best place for oil to absorb was the bottoms of the feet, palms of the hands and tips of the ears. Warm the oil up first by rubbing the hands together. Then, after she used it, she should smell it from her hands by putting them over her nose to get more of the aroma into her system.

It was a tiny bottle, but CK didn't care. It was very strong, and she planned to use all of it at once.

"Here goes," said CK, as she poured most of the bottle into her left palm (also her receiving palm). She rubbed her hands together to warm the oil and smeared it on the bottom of her feet and then around her ears. The smell was extremely strong, like a flower shop on Valentine's Day. For good measure, she also rubbed the extra oil on her chest to engage with her heart chakra. That should bring her vibration up! Finally, she put her hands up to her face, covering her cheeks, nose and even most of her whiskers and breathed in deeply so that all of the essence of the Rose flower seeped into her system.

What an amazing feeling! CK felt lightheaded after sniffing the Rose oil. Thankfully she was already sitting down, or she would have needed to find a seat! Her energy shot up, and she felt tingles all over her body coming from the scent. She looked around, and she could now hear the trees just a little bit more. She could also just make out three small outlines hovering above her head.

"Celeste! Prog! Nana Whiskers! Is that you!?!" CK screamed. She couldn't hear their answer, as they were still too faint. All she could see was a ripple in the air which looked like heat coming off a hot pavement in the summer. In her heart, she knew it was them, but she still could not see or communicate with them directly. CK looked around for the portal. It still was not in view, though she could see a slight vibration on the side of the mountain, similar to the one she saw floating around her head.

"That's it! We are getting close!" she exclaimed with excitement. *What else? What else?* She thought.

Then CK remembered that she had the article. She dug back into her bag from the shop and pulled out the magazine, flaunting an article on how to raise your vibration inside.

She quickly flipped to the article and found the top 15 list. Anxiously CK read, "Here are our top 15 things you can do to raise your vibration..."*

Fifteen - Say "no" to things and people who drain your energy

I've already done that, thought CK. *I live in Joy-Ville, for goodness' sake!*

The article continued ...

Fourteen – Minimize Technology Toys – put down the computer, cell phones, other devices

CK thought for a moment. They did have a few entertainment devices in Joy-Ville but nothing compared to what she had seen here. And she would be perfectly happy to give up that reality TV show they watched last night! That was terrible!

Next! CK yelled in her mind.

---

* Countdown to a high vibration inspired by a blog posted from Rebecca Campbell

Thirteen – Reduce clutter – rooms, drawers, closets, workspace – clean it out

A good idea, CK thought, *but that won't help me now. I already live very simply, so perhaps that is one of the reasons we can maintain our vibration in Joy-Ville.*

CK continued; she was running out of time and out of ideas.

Twelve – Live in the Present Moment

Ah, that's a good one, thought CK. *I did that coming back into the forest, and I work on that one almost every day. Being present allows you to notice the beauty and magnificence of things around you and truly be with yourself and others wherever you are.*

CK kept reading.

Eleven – Notice the beauty all around you

Perfect! Thought CK. *That goes right along with being present and in the moment. The trees, flowers, animals and other souls are all so wonderful when you take the time to notice them.*

Ten – Go barefoot, especially walking on soil

That's a great idea! CK took off her shoes and began to dig her toes into the soft earth, feeling the cool moisture run through her toes and over her heels. It felt great and gave CK a feeling of calm, combined with an energy boost.

With her feet now firmly pushed down into the dirt, CK continued.

Nine – Eat living foods that are raw (like wheatgrass)

I would LOVE to do this one, CK thought. *But unfortunately I don't have any food around, so we'll skip it for now.* She continued.

Eight – Be nice to someone, especially a stranger you don't know

I did that already! Hurray! CK thought back to her conversation with Ralph and the warm feeling she got helping him and how much she enjoyed just chatting and telling him about meditation. He said it was a blessing, but CK knew it was more of a blessing to her.

Seven – Breathe deeply and meditate

Perfect! I did that one too, CK thought, though she was starting to be slightly concerned she was running out of numbers.

Six – Burn sage or use sea salt to clear away negative energy, or even swim in the ocean

Yep – CHECK! She thought as she remembered the heavy smell of sage on her clothes.

Five – Be thankful; consider writing in a gratitude journal every day

Nice, that's a good one. I have been doing that a lot today. CK once again offered up a prayer and thoughts of gratitude for the wonderful experience and her expectation and thanks for going home.

Four – Dance!

Another good one, we'll come back to that, thought CK.

Three - Laugh and hang out with high vibration friends

Not right now unless I can get my vibration high enough to laugh with Celeste and Nana Whiskers, though I don't think I have ever seen Prog laugh.

Two - Listen to or sing happy, positive music

Perfect! I LOVE to sing! Singing makes my heart so happy! CK was very excited by the idea of singing. She knew that was something she could do well and it would make a big difference in her mood.

And last, on the list of the top ways to raise your vibration was…

One – Engage in positive thinking and intent – Choose Joy!

I choose Joy, thought CK. *My intent is to be positive and choose Joy, regardless.* With this thought, CK's heart began to soar. She could feel the positive energy and emotion welling up inside her as she was also thankful for the beautiful joy that was coming in.

CK looked around at the portal. She could see its outline shimmering in the distance against the stone wall, but she was still not at the right frequency to be able to pass through. She needed to do something, and quickly, as the sun was just beginning to set over the trees.

CK scanned back over the article to decide where to focus her efforts. What would give her the biggest "bang for her vibrational buck," to use a phrase from this dimension? *That would definitely be the singing!* She decided, and her heart leaped a beat. But what would she sing? What would have a high vibration and lift her up quickly?

CK heard a soft voice belonging to Celeste faintly whisper, "The ABCs of Affirmation."

Super! Thought CK. *Thank you, Celeste!*

This was a song she had written long ago and still sang on a regular basis. One of the ways of changing things in life and stating what is true is by saying, or in this case singing, affirmations. Affirmations are positive statements that are regularly repeated with great emotion to let the Universe know what a being intends. It's a beautiful way to manifest and co-create the world along with the Universe. This song was a way to remind CK and others of how to use affirmations in their life.

CK stood up and cleared her throat, which by this time was quite dry. She decided the best way to sing this song would be to sing it loudly and do a little dance along with it to increase the vibration as well. Hopefully, by singing this happy song, she would raise her vibration enough to be in alignment with the energy of portal.

CK took a few dance steps and began to sing in front of the space where she saw the shimmer of energy against the wall of Whale Mountain.

Slowly she began…

"From the ABCs of affirmations, I do draw my declarations. Bringing my intent to life helps me overcome my strife.

Sing a song of who you are, and that future is not far; Thoughts create reality, showing who we're meant to be.

I choose my words with care and light, making sure they are just right,

So in my life, the good I see, is that which I have brought to me."

As CK finished the first stanza, the energy and pace of the song picked up dramatically...

"So...I...am...Happy and I'm Healthy, and I'm Wealthy, and I'm Wise...I am pure Love and Joy.

I am Peaceful, I am Present, I am Safe, and I'm Secure...I am pure Love and Joy.

I am thankful, so grateful, for my blessings every day, from the Angels, Guides and Guardians who help me on my way!"

As CK finished the first pass through the song, she could feel the positive energy rise from her heart. She could see the spinning portal getting brighter and she could see more of it coming into her vision. She could see the outlines of Celeste, Prog and Nana Whiskers getting darker as well, and she could just make out the pink spirals on Celeste's heart-shaped body, and she was certain she could see Progs' scowl.

"Keep singing!" shouted Celeste. "It's working!"

Cosmic Kitty started the refrain again, this time singing louder and with greater emotion and love than before. CK belted out the words, boldly pronouncing the words "I AM" before each statement to give it more impact.

I Am Happy, I Am Healthy, I Am Wealthy, I Am Wise...I Am pure Love and Joy.

I Am Peaceful, I Am Present, I Am Safe, I Am Secure...I Am pure Love and Joy.

I Am thankful, so grateful, for my blessings every day, from the Angels, Guides and Guardians who help me on my way!"

This time, as CK finished her last verse, the spinning portal came into full view. She could see directly through the portal, which still looked like the eye of the whale. On the other side, she could see her friends, the trees, waving their branches in the wind, playing with some birds who were jumping between their branches.

Home! Thought CK with great excitement.

She had done it! She had raised her vibration enough to be able to see through the portal back into Joy-Ville, sitting in the fifth dimension.

"Great job, CK!" came the cheers from her spiritual posse. "You did it! You found the portal again and raised your vibration back up!"

CK turned to see Celeste, Prog, and Nana Whiskers. She had never been so happy to see such familiar faces! She threw her arms around the group and pulled them in for a hug. It was an odd hug, to say the least, given they were only about six inches tall, except Nana Whiskers, who was floating beside them slightly larger. But CK didn't care. She was just so happy to see them she thought her heart would nearly burst with joy and excitement. Even Prog managed a smile when no one was looking. He and Celeste also gave personal thanks to the Archangels, Ascended Masters, Gods, Goddesses and other beings of light in the Universe for helping to get CK home safely. They needed all the help they could get too! As far as cosmic support goes, sometimes it takes a Village!

"Now hurry," said Nana Whiskers, "let's get you home!"

"But I won't be able to see you back home," protested CK.

"That's true," confirmed Celeste, "but now that you know who we are, I'm sure you will be able to hear us and see the signs we leave to help you on your journey. You see, CK, we are ALWAYS with you. We never leave you. We just communicate in different ways depending on the situation. The more you look and listen for us, and the more you acknowledge when we help you, the greater your power to feel, hear and even see us will become. You have great power that you are just now starting to use. One day you will understand the role you have decided to play in this lifetime, for yourself and for Joy-Ville," Celeste continued.

CK listened. She didn't really know what Celeste was talking about or what power and decision she had made in this lifetime. But what she DID know was that she was ready to get home to her friends.

CK took one last look around her world in the third dimension. With her vibration raised, she once again noticed how hazy and dirty the sky looked here, and how everything had a dull color to it compared to her world. She gave her spiritual posse another hug and kiss since it would be hard to see them again once she walked through the portal.

As she glanced around, CK didn't see anyone else in the area. It was a good thing too, because if anyone had been watching her, they would have seen a funny-looking girl with red hair walk straight into the side of a mountain and disappear without a trace. That would have been hard to explain and in some families might even cause a trip to the doctor's office for tests! But thankfully, no one saw Cosmic Kitty disappear back into the fifth dimension except the trees, birds, squirrels and chipmunks, who sent their love for saving their forest.

Chapter 16

THE OTHER SIDE

As CK came through the other side of Whale Mountain, she breathed a deep sigh of relief. She was home. It was time to find her friends! Surely they must be very worried about her, having been gone more than a full day! CK quickly walked back through the trees which made up the forest by Whale Mountain. These were the same trees she had just worked to save in the third dimension. She bowed to them as she hurried past, anxious to see her friends. They waved their branches at her in greeting, wondering why she was in such a rush, and then went back to playing with the birds.

CK found the path she had followed to get to Whale Mountain, where she had been daydreaming about Starlight. How funny the dirt path now felt under her feet after walking on so much hard concrete. And oddly enough, this path was in the same place as the sidewalk that went into the city from her walk earlier in the day. A strange feeling of familiarity came over CK as she realized she was walking in the same direction to get back to her village that she had walked to get into the city when she went to find herself in the third dimension. Amazing how many things were so different, yet some things were just the same, like the direction home. As CK walked along the path headed back toward the pond, Timrek's banjo came into range again. He was STILL singing the same song!

Oh, Timrek, thought Cosmic Kitty, *you need a new song. You were singing that one yesterday when I left!* But it was his favorite song, CK thought, so it made sense. As she thought back to her own song which just brought her home, "The ABCs of Affirmation," she recalled that she used to sing that one every single day for years. Now she just sang it about once every few weeks as a reminder. But when a song comes from your heart and speaks your truth, the heart will repeat the song over and over again. It just wants to come out. So she knew how Timrek felt.

As CK got closer to the pond, she could see that Sunny was still lighting up the afternoon in the same way he had been the day before. The fish and turtles were still playing tag, and the frogs were jumping into the water off the lily pads. She came up to Timrek. He was still sitting on the same log where he had been daydreaming of Rainbow Connections the day before.

"Hi CK," said Timrek. "Back from your walk so quickly? That was fast. Usually, you travel a bit farther on a nice afternoon like this one."

CK's mouth dropped open in shock and surprise. *A fast walk?!?* She thought. *Poor Timrek, he must be very confused. He obviously doesn't realize what day it is.*

"Actually," started CK, "I have been gone for more than a day. It was one of the longest walks I have ever taken! I ended up going through this spinning portal at Whale Mountain that took me into a third dimension version of our world. It was strange and unique. Very different than our world here. They don't have a good relationship with nature, and they live in these big steel and cement buildings. I met myself, my spirit Guides and even my Grandmother!" CK blurted out.

Timrek just looked at her. He had never known CK to make up stories, though she was extremely creative and quite a good singer. But if she wanted to branch out into books and fables, that was great! A new author in Joy-Ville would be very welcome!

"That sounds like a super storyline, CK!" Timrek replied. "That would make a great book or movie! You should write it down. No wonder you came back so fast – you must be looking for pen and paper to capture the ideas."

CK didn't understand why Timrek did not believe her and thought this was in her mind. Didn't she disappear from Joy-Ville for an entire day? Weren't friends out looking for her, concerned because she had disappeared?

CK thanked Timrek for his suggestion on the book and decided to find someone else who would be looking for her.

She walked quickly around the pond, heading back to the village. When she arrived, she found Lois sitting outside her hut. She was making clothing from yarn and fabric, something she loved to do and did most days. Lois would make clothes for everyone in the village, and usually, she made too much. Today was no exception, as she was knitting away on a lovely shirt with big, bright orange buttons.

"Lois, I'm back," said CK, slightly out of breath from walking so quickly back from the pond.

"Oh CK, lovely to see you, my darling. Did you have a nice walk this afternoon? The Sun has been doing his best to warm us all up after the cloudy morning," Lois said, not missing a beat in her flawless knitting routine.

For the second time, CK's jaw dropped open, and nothing came out. "What day is it?" CK asked.

"Why, it's Friday, of course," replied Lois. "Why do you ask?"

"Friday!?!" exclaimed CK. "How can it be Friday? That is the same day I left Joy-Ville and went to see Katherine in the schoolyard! How can that be?"

CK thanked Lois and left. She needed to find answers.

That was strange, thought Lois. But she thought nothing more of it and returned her focus back to her sewing.

CK decided that to get to the bottom of this, only one person could help her – or one reptile, to be more precise. And off she went to find him.

Mr. Tortoise sat outside the entrance to his home. He lived in a large hole buried deep in the Earth. His home was very spacious, and the kids would visit him inside, but today he was sitting on a rock outside his house warming his shell (and his bones) in Sunny's bright rays.

Mr. Tortoise had a most unusual shell. It had spirals all over it, a bit different from the other turtles who lived in Joy-Ville. Cosmic Kitty had never noticed the patterns of his shell before. As she got closer to him, she realized that the pattern was the same as the set of spirals she saw on Celeste! What a very interesting observation indeed! She would have to ask him about that one day. Perhaps he knew Celeste as well? But for now, Cosmic Kitty needed to figure out what happened. Why did no one seem to notice that she had been gone and why was it still Friday here?

As CK walked up, Mr. Tortoise pulled down his glasses to see her better. He didn't actually need glasses to read, as his vision was perfect, but he liked the way they looked and found it funny that they were called "tortoiseshell" in color. He had picked them up many centuries ago when Joy-Ville was quite young and still evolving. No one needed glasses anymore, but Mr. Tortoise kept them as a souvenir from a different time, way before most of today's inhabitants, or even their parents, were ever born. And since these also had good sun protection, it was a bonus.

"Hello CK," he said in a calm and soothing voice as she approached.

"Mr. T," CK began breathlessly. "I am so confused, and I need your help, please!"

Mr. Tortoise just nodded slowly at her. Just being around him made her feel calmer and more peaceful. He gave off that sort of energy.

"Sit down, CK, and breathe," instructed Mr. Tortoise, "this can wait two minutes while you catch your breath and relax," he said.

CK hated it when Mr. Tortoise was right, and he usually was. She had become so anxious and wrapped up in understanding why no one had missed her that her chest was tight and she didn't feel well. She was also thirsty and hungry from her travels. Mr. Tortoise could sense this.

"Why don't you get some water? I have some nice fresh vegetables and fruit here as well. You look like you could use something to eat," he encouraged.

CK knew he was right, even if she did not want to admit it. She walked over to a tray and pitcher he had set up, poured herself a glass of water and slurped it down quickly. Sheepishly she refilled the glass and drank half of it down again. She then took a clay plate from his tray and put some fresh carrots, eggplant, and spinach on it, along with an apple and a peach. Mr. Tortoise only ate raw fruits and veggies. That is one of the reasons he had lived so long, or so he told anyone who asked. CK ate a few bites of the apple and some of the spinach. She took a deep breath and sat down beside Mr. Tortoise. They were quiet for a few minutes as CK ate a few more bites of her food and tried to collect her thoughts for how she might explain all of this to Mr. Tortoise. He waited patiently for CK to rest and eat. It would all come out in good time, as it was meant to. Meanwhile, he continued to enjoy the beautiful sun rays of the day.

As CK ate and drank, she began to feel much better. The nagging hunger and thirst died away, and the memories from her trip started to lose their sharp, urgent edge. But she still had so many questions!

CK took another deep breath and began. "Mr. T, has anyone been looking for me today?" she started again.

"Not that I know of," said Mr. Tortoise, "but you know I don't get involved in people's daily life unless they ask me to. Why?"

"Well, I went for a walk earlier today. And I walked pretty far, all the way to Whale Mountain. When I got there, I found a spinning portal on the side of the rock."

CK stopped to judge Mr. Tortoise's reaction. He just nodded for her to continue.

"I could see through the rock into another world, so I went through. I ended up in our world, but in a different dimension. It was the third dimension according to my Guides, who I could also see."

CK stopped again. "Go on," encouraged Mr. Tortoise, "I believe you."

"So I ended up finding myself in the third dimension. I was a girl named Katherine. She was mean to me in the beginning, but then we got to be friends, and she helped me stop the destruction of some trees that were going to be knocked down. I even got to use Reiki to heal another child who had been hurt."

CK stopped for the third time. "Interesting," was all Mr. Tortoise would say, so she continued.

"I even had to stay overnight because it was too late to come back. Katherine's family was mean, and they had terrible food and loud, negative shows they called entertainment. So when I finally got ready to come home, I couldn't go through the portal. I couldn't find it because my vibration had dropped too low. By that time it was Saturday afternoon, so I had to find some help to get my vibration up to come back home."

"I see," was all Mr. Tortoise would offer, though his body language and energy told CK he believed her.

"Oh, wait! I'll show you!" CK emptied her pockets. She brought out three stones, including a very rare Moldavite. Mr. Tortoise was impressed. He hadn't seen Moldavite in years. She also pulled out green paper with numbers on it that she had used for money. On seeing this, his eyes lit up. Mr. Tortoise knew EXACTLY what she was holding.

"I haven't seen this since I was a kid!" he exclaimed, in the most excited voice a 1,000-plus-year-old turtle could muster. "It was used for making exchanges for food, clothes and other items when you didn't have something to trade. That was a time when people did not share the way they do today in Joy-Ville. Now we all do what is needed to help each other and share our talents. But when I was a kid, it was not always that way everywhere. This green paper was used by many people to 'purchase' things they needed or wanted. That was a very negative time in our history before we were even called 'Joy-Ville'," he explained.

"So you believe me?" asked Cosmic Kitty.

"Yes CK, I do," he replied.

"So why did no one miss me when I didn't come home until Saturday evening?" CK asked.

"Because today is still Friday," Mr. Tortoise explained. "You haven't been missing since you just went for a walk an hour or two ago."

"But how can that be?" asked CK, confused.

"One thing you have to understand about our friend Time," explained Mr. Tortoise, "is that it is completely irrelevant. Time does not exist in the cosmic sense. We use it to help us manage our physical worlds, of course. Otherwise, we would be in a bit of chaos. But in the bigger scheme of things, everything is happening in parallel. So even though you spent time in the third dimension, you came right back into this world at the same time you left. That is why no one had missed you yet."

"Oh" was all CK could say. She didn't understand how this might work or why time did not really exist. That had not been her experience, so even though she was open to the idea, it did not sink in for her as an actual truth. But Mr. Tortoise had never given her bad information in the past, so she decided it was probably true.

"So no one knew I was gone?" CK asked to clarify her position.

"That is correct," stated Mr. Tortoise, who could now see that CK looked extremely tired and seemed to be drooping.

CK had so much she wanted to tell Mr. Tortoise and so many questions she wanted to ask. But she decided that perhaps they would have to wait for another day. The adrenaline rush from saving the trees, meeting Katherine, lowering and then raising her vibration, dealing with Madam Zorba, meeting Ralph, performing Reiki in the third dimension and finally finding her way home was too much for the moment. She was exhausted. Her body was rebelling. It was ready for bed.

Mr. Tortoise could see the conflict on CK's face. Her whiskers twitched, wanting to share more of her adventures, but her eyes told Mr. Tortoise she was one tired girl and fighting against sleep.

"I think it's time for you to go, CK," offered Mr. Tortoise. "I am quite tired today, and I need my rest," he continued. "I want to hear all about your stories and adventures and everything that happened while you were gone. But I am ready for a nap. If it is ok with you, can we pick back up tomorrow and talk about this more?" he asked.

CK was very grateful for his recommendation. She agreed to come back the next day and tell Mr. Tortoise every detail of her great adventure in the third dimension. But for now, she would head home herself, and into her warm bed. The blankets made by Lois would be just perfect, and she knew she would sleep well tonight!

"Don't forget your 'money' and your stones," Mr. Tortoise called after her. CK returned to her seat to pick up her souvenirs from the third dimension. She couldn't wait to show them to her friends.

But for now, sleep was the only priority. CK slowly walked home. Moon Man was now coming up over the horizon as Sunny retired for the day.

"Hello Moon Man," called CK in a sleepy voice.

"Good evening, CK!" he called back. "You look very tired. Go to bed, and I will ask Starlight to send you some sweet dreams!" CK blew him a kiss of thanks.

She wandered into her home, a large hut built into the side of a mountain. She got another glass of water to put on her bedside table. She brushed her teeth and washed her face. She did not have enough energy for a bath tonight. Sleep was the only priority.

CK crawled into bed, between the warm blankets and pillows. As she drifted off to sleep, her mind wondered what other doorways that portal might open. Perhaps there were other places she might be able to visit? Would she see Celeste and Prog and Nana Whiskers again?

And as her friends Moon Man and Starlight brought the evening into full view, Cosmic Kitty began to dream. She had colorful visions and ideas that perhaps, just perhaps, the portal might help her find yet another path to a whole new world and a grand new adventure, but it would have to be on another day.

The End

ACKNOWLEDGMENTS AND AUTHOR'S COMMENTS

I have put this section at the end because this is intended to be a book for kids. However, it is my hope that anyone who picks up Cosmic Kitty will find some value in her story. To that end, I wanted to share some of where this information has come from and also give proper thanks to those who have been involved in its development.

Cosmic Kitty could not have been written without the amazing guidance I have received throughout its creation. I have been doodling CK and Joy-Ville since I was seven years old, in Columbus, Georgia. However, until 2015, she did not have a name, much less a voice or description. I have been on my journey of self-awareness, mindfulness, and consciousness for many years, but only in recent times has it sped up significantly. This awakening happens for many people as we get into our late 30s and 40s. If it happens to you, I hope you will embrace it!

Over the last several years I have taken courses, read books, seen shows, listened to Ted Talks and videos, talked with friends, met with readers and had many different resources just "happen" across my path that have helped with my journey and personal development. There are way too many to name them all, but I would like to thank and provide a reference here for some of the content in this book.

First and foremost, I thank God, my spirit guides, the angels, ascended masters and other spirits who have helped to create this material. For the most part, this book was channeled. I had no idea where the story would go, as there was no outline for it and I did not know who the characters would be. Bits and pieces came in dreams over the last year, but until I actually sat down and started typing, I honestly did not know the plot. At times I even argued with my guides (in my mind) on how things like dimensions and vibration would work. Thankfully they had great patience in explaining it to me and helping me to understand the points they were trying to get me to make. I am humbled and honored for the love, support, and information provided to me by these amazing beings of light. I am forever grateful for your presence in my life.

I would also like to thank **my family**, who have been a huge support. I always have their unconditional love. All they have ever truly wanted for me is to be happy even when they had concerns I was getting a bit too "woo-woo" at times. (Yes, Dad, the stones are still under your chair.) Thank you for the Love and Support you have always shown **Mom, Dad, Jay, and Kristen**!! And for those cute kids to whom this book is dedicated, **James** and **Adair**.

As with any great journey, the resources I needed along my path have shown up without fail. These thanks are in no particular order, as they have all provided amazing support in this process.

Cosmic Kitty found her voice when she came out during a Soul Sensuality painting retreat, facilitated by Julie Stuart in summer of 2015. Painting and finally naming Cosmic Kitty, or CK, triggered a floodgate of knowledge and creativity. It was also the first time CK had ever been drawn in color and with an aura around her. Thank you for helping me to remember and bring back my inner child so that CK could speak her voice again. I could not properly hear her until we painted her in that retreat, through pushing me to pull out her story. From that point, I knew she needed to be a book. Thank you, Julie!

In that same month, I started two additional classes, both of which gave me profound insights into this process.

Carl Woodall and **Sherry Davenport** taught a five-month psychic development program using the Sandy Anastasi PD program. Through it, I learned how to connect directly to my spirit guides and have even managed to chat with a few departed grandparents of friends as part of the process. They taught me that intuitive development is a muscle that must be worked, just like any other activity or exercise. But we must also be extremely mindful to work only in the light and with the protection of our Arch Angels, and always for the highest good of those involved. Thank you, Carl and Sherry!

Sherry Davenport has also played a large role in supporting me throughout the creation of this book as well. In addition to the very practical editorial and website support and the great metaphysical classes she teaches, Sherry has been a huge cheerleader for Cosmic Kitty. She helped me to validate I was on the right path and often provided the additional guidance and motivation I needed to keep moving forward. I learned that even when you have Divine help on a project, ya still have to do the work! Thank you, Sherry! You are a God send, literally!

In the same month as the painting retreat and the first Psychic Development class, I also started a new course that completely changed the way I think about dimensions and energy forever.

The month before, I was extremely fortunate to take Reiki one and two from a talented and highly attuned Reiki Master, **Kumari Mullin**. But as I found out, there was so much more for me to learn from her. In July 2015, I started a 36 week (3-course) adventure with Kumari and a group of other students, working with new energetics coming down from higher dimensions. My understanding of cosmic energies, ascended masters, vibrations and the transformation our planet is under-going became more clear for me in this process. I truly believe that one of the reasons Cosmic Kitty is now coming out is because she is meant to help the next generation to understand what we CAN achieve if we are open to working with higher vibration energies and letting go of fear. Kumari's Divine Human course and the subsequent discussions at Aruna in Florida have helped me to understand our potential when we choose joy and choose to live, think, and love in a higher dimension. Thank you, Kumari! The journey continues!

I would also like to thank **Kisha Lee Crawford**, here in Atlanta. I have been attending Kisha's Women's meditation classes for almost two years, since moving to the Atlanta area. She has shown me that meditation is not just about creating space and a place for quiet (which it is), but also about using meditation to manifest and create intentions for what you want in your life. Many times Cosmic Kitty has been put into a golden ball of light in class and sent off for manifestation with the Universe, and now she is here! Thank you, Kisha!

Kisha's meditation classes introduced me to Oracle Cards, specifically working with Goddesses. However, after taking Psychic Development with Carl and Sherry, as serendipity would have it, **Karen Moore Thomson** just happened to be teaching a Tarot class that winter as well. I was taking the class just for fun and to learn more about it, but didn't realize how much I would enjoy Tarot reading! I learned a great deal from Karen and used some of that knowledge here in the book as well. I still pull Tarot cards regularly for self and others, and every time I am still amazed at the accuracy and support that comes through from guides who are using them to help us. Thank you, Karen!

My passion and love for stones started back in early 2014 while I was still living in Columbus Georgia (for the second time in my life). I went in for a massage with no idea my world would explode with weekly stone meditations, intention grid classes, and energy work. Thank you, **Debbie Blake-Knox**! I still have and cherish the stones you taught to me. I miss our weekly stone meditations, but I know they are a blessing to many others in your area!

Although it may seem odd to some, I would also like to thank **Oprah Winfrey**. Her Super Soul Sunday and Super Soul Sessions provided amazing inspiration and refuge for me in times when I needed more positive messages in my life. Oprah has changed the dialogue on topics like these. She made it "ok" to talk about energy, manifestation, intentions and chakras in open discussions around the country, even in corporations. She has opened me up to new books and authors I didn't even know, and greatly advanced the topic of how we raise our consciousness and vibration in this world. Thank you, Oprah!

Finally, I would like to thank **Dan McNeal**. We lost Dan in 2001, and his death was one of the key reasons I started my spiritual journey. He set me on this path of seeking which has not only brought this book to reality but changed my life forever. Thank you, Dan, I love and miss you!

There are so many others I could thank, but then I would never stop. So many friends and colleagues ask about the book regularly and talk about metaphysical ideas with me, sharing their experiences. I send you all hugs, love, and light! Thank you!

If you are still with me to the end of this section, I thank you as well. It is truly a gift to have people and community around us who can provide support and love as we develop our spirit. Thank you, gentle reader, for taking the time to spend with Cosmic Kitty. I thank you most of all, as it is you who can help us to bring some of these Fifth Dimension thoughts into our Third Dimension world. Namaste.

With Love,

Shan

For more dialogue on these topics, check out shangill.com.

ABOUT THE AUTHOR

S han Gill is a practitioner and student of metaphysical studies, a passion that fuels her work as a life strategist and coach, helping others bridge the world of today and live their highest truth. She brings business and consciousness together through her 20+ years of corporate experience, including several years in product development for The Disney Corporation in Hong Kong. Her passion for Disney characters and their stories, along with a desire to help people of all ages easily understand and access metaphysical and dimensional elements of their world, has led her to bring Cosmic Kitty to life.

In addition to her corporate experience, Shan has a unique and complementary blend of traditional and metaphysical training. Not only is she certified in leadership facilitation, intuitive development, reiki and tarot, she also has her BA from St. Andrews College in Laurinburg, NC and her MBA from Georgetown University in Washington DC. More information at shangill.com.

Printed in the United States
By Bookmasters